DUPLEX

Also by Kathryn Davis

Labrador
The Girl Who Trod on a Loaf
Hell
The Walking Tour
Versailles
The Thin Place

Duplex

A Novel

KATHRYN DAVIS

GRAYWOLF PRESS

This publication is made possible, in part, by the voters of Minnesota through a Minnesota State Arts Board Operating Support grant, thanks to a legislative appropriation from the arts and cultural heritage fund, and through a grant from the National Endowment for the Arts. Significant support has also been provided by Target, the McKnight Foundation, Amazon.com, and other generous contributions from foundations, corporations, and individuals. To these organizations and individuals we offer our heartfelt thanks.

Published by Graywolf Press
250 Third Avenue North, Suite 600
Minneapolis, Minnesota 55401

www.graywolfpress.org

Published in the United States of America

Printed in Canada

ISBN 978-1-55597-653-8

2 4 6 8 9 7 5 3 1
First Graywolf Printing, 2013

Library of Congress Control Number: 2013936988

Cover design: Anne Davis and Sarah Purdy

Cover art: Bo Bartlett, *Lifeboat*, 1998. Oil on linen. 80 × 100 inches. Courtesy of the artist and P.P.O.W. Gallery, New York.

For Anne Davis, Peggy Reavey & Rosemary Sedgwick

(my first generation of girls)

DUPLEX

Body-without-Soul

IT WAS A SUBURBAN STREET, ONE BLOCK LONG, THE houses made of brick and built to last like the third little pig's. Sycamore trees had been planted at regular intervals along the curb and the curbs themselves sparkled; I think the concrete was mixed with mica in it. I think when it was new the street couldn't help but draw attention to itself, inviting envy.

Miss Vicks lived at the lower end of the street, in number 49. Most of the other houses had families living in them but she was by herself, a woman of about fifty, slim and still attractive, with a red short-haired dachshund. By the time she moved in, the sycamore trees had grown so large they had enormous holes cut through their crowns to make room for all the wires.

She was a real woman; you could tell by the way she didn't have to move her head from side to side to take in sound. Every day she and the dachshund went for three walks, the first early in the morning, the second in the late afternoon, and the third after dinner, when the blue-green lights of the scows, those slow-moving heralds of melancholy, would begin to appear in the night sky. The little dog would sniff around the feet of the sycamores and as it did she would stand there paralyzed as all the Miss Vickses that had ever been layered themselves inside her, one atop the other and increasingly small, forming a great laminate like tree rings around heartwood.

Bedtime, the end of summer. The street was filled with children, many of them the same children she'd soon be welcoming into her classroom. School was about to start. "Heads up!" the boys yelled when a car appeared, interrupting their play; the girls sat making deals on the porch stoops, cigar boxes of trading cards and stickers in their laps. Meanwhile the darkness welled up so gradually the only way anyone could tell night had fallen was the fireflies, prickling like light on water. The parents were inside, keeping an eye on the children but also drinking highballs. Fireflies like falling stars, the tree trunks narrow as the girls' waists.

Occasionally something different happened. One girl pasted a diadem of gold star stickers to her forehead and wandered from her stoop to get closer to where one of the boys stood bending slightly forward, his hands on his knees, nervously waiting for another boy to hit the ball. This waiting boy was Eddie, who lived at the opposite end of the street from Miss Vicks, in number 24; the girl was Mary, who lived in the house attached to hers. Sometimes Miss Vicks could hear Mary practicing the piano through the living room wall—"Für Elise" with the same mistake in the same spot, over and over. A fingering problem, simple enough to fix if only the parents would give the girl some lessons.

Headlights appeared; the boys scattered. Mary remained standing at the curb in her plaid shorts and white T-shirt, balanced like a stork on one leg. The car was expensive and silver-gray and driven by the sorcerer Body-without-Soul. Miss Vicks didn't recognize him right away because like everyone else she was blinded by the headlights. The headlights turned the lenses of her and Mary's spectacles to blazing disks of hammered gold so neither one of them could see the street, the trees, the houses—anything at all, really—and the next minute the car was gone. It was only after the taillights had disappeared around the corner that Miss Vicks realized she had recognized the license plate: 1511MV, a prime, followed by her initials.

Early in their romance the sorcerer told her he took this for a sign. Miss Vicks was not a superstitious person but like most people she was susceptible to flattery. She and her dog had been walking through the ruined gardens of the Woodard Estate when the sorcerer suddenly appeared on the path in front of them, a tall figure in a finely tailored suit, his shadow cast behind him, his face gold like melted sun. It was as if he'd been expecting her; when he circled her wrist with his fingers to draw her close to ask her name, she felt the life inside her leap up from everywhere, shocking, like a hatch of mayflies. He said he'd been hunting but she didn't see a gun anywhere. "The animal kingdom," he said, disparagingly, giving her little dog a nudge with the toe of his pointed shoe. He was a Woodard—it made sense that he would be there even after the place had fallen into desuetude.

Now her dog was raising his hackles. Miss Vicks could feel him tugging on the leash, bravely holding the soft red flags of his ears aloft and out to either side like banderillas.

"Has anyone seen Eddie?" Mary asked.

"He disappeared," Roy Duffy told her, but he was joking.

Everyone knew how Eddie was—here one minute, gone the next. He was a small, jumpy boy; he moved so fast it was as if he got where he was headed before anyone ever noticed he'd left where he started out. Besides, they were all disappearing into their houses—it was only the beginning. The game was over; the next day school started. When the crest of one wave of light met the trough of another the result was blackness.

Tonight, as every night, from inside number 24 came the

sound of Eddie's parents playing canasta. "I'll meld *you!*" said his mother, raucous with the joy of competition. The two of them were sitting on either side of the card table they set up in the living room each night after dinner, but you couldn't see them, only hear their voices, the front bow window filled with a lush ivy plant in an Italian cachepot.

Miss Vicks watched Mary start down the street.

"Goodnight, Miss Vicks," Mary said.

"See you tomorrow, Mary," she replied.

In the brick houses the clocks kept ticking away the time, chipping off pieces of it, some big ones piling thick and heavy under the brass weights of the grandfather clock in Eddie's parents' hallway, others so small and fast even the round watchful eyes of the cat clock in Mary's parents' kitchen couldn't track their flight. The crickets were rubbing their hind legs together, unrolling that endless band of sound that when combined with the sound of the sycamore trees tossing their heads in the heat-thickened breeze could cause even a girl as unsentimental as Mary to feel like she'd just left something behind on the porch stoop she couldn't bear to live without.

Miss Vicks waited on the grass verge in front of number 24 for her dog to complete his business. He always deposited it in the same place between the curb and the sidewalk; she would scoop it into a bag and then it would get carried into the heavens by a scow. The street was empty, the materialization of the silver-gray car having driven everyone inside.

Thinking of the sorcerer, Miss Vicks became aroused. He had his way of doing things. When he drove he liked to rest his one hand lightly on the wheel and leave the other free to stroke her between the legs. His fingernails were perfect ovals like flower petals, and he had eyes so black and so deep-set sometimes she thought they weren't eyes but holes.

Even when they seemed to be looking at the road she knew what he was seeing was himself.

He'd been with a woman he left to be with her, and another woman before that, and before that many other women—Miss Vicks had heard the stories. Once she saw him escorting a blonde woman into a restaurant, his hand at the small of the woman's back, and to her shame she realized her jealousy was nothing compared with her vicarious sense of excitement at the thought of his touch. He wasn't promiscuous though, or so he claimed the one time she confronted him. He was just having difficulty finding the right woman.

"I'm not like you," he'd told her, as if that were justification enough. They were lying on her bed with all the lights on, the way he liked it, and he was slipping one hand under her expensive Italian camisole while guiding her lips to meet his with the other. Of course she knew he was right, though probably not the way he meant it. The sorcerer could make things appear or he could make them vanish; he could make them turn into other things or he could make them vibrate at unprecedented frequencies, the explanation for his great success in bed. It was only *things*, though. When the sorcerer looked at the street he saw it crawling with souls like the earth with worms. It was no secret that even the lowliest of the unruly, uncontainable beings living there could partake of love's mystery, and his envious rage knew no bounds.

The dachshund had finished and was kicking up grass blades with his hind legs. From far to the west came a rumble of thunder; Miss Vicks grew aware of the changing temperature of the air. In this latitude summer storms moved in quickly and did a lot of damage before moving away. "Come on," she said to the dog, who seemed frozen in place, staring at nothing. Dark spots appeared on the sidewalk, a few at first and then more and more. She yanked the leash. Face it, she told herself. The man is a beast. You'd be better off without him. She could hear windows closing, the sound of Mr. O'Toole yelling instructions at Mrs. O'Toole. The back door—something about the back door swinging in the wind.

On the sidewalk outside number 37 (another prime) came the first flash of lightning, just a flash like a huge light had been turned on; for a moment it was as if it was possible to see everything in the world. Then there was another flash, this one displayed like an X-ray image of the central nervous system above the even-numbered houses on the other side of the street. Everyone knew the family inside number 37 were robots. Mr. XA, Mrs. XA, Cindy XA, Carol XA—when you saw them outside the house they looked like people. Carol had been in Miss Vicks's class the previous year and she had been an excellent if uninspired student; Cindy would be in her class starting tomorrow. The question of how to teach—or even whether to teach—a robot came up from time to time among the teachers. No one had a good answer.

By the time Miss Vicks got to number 49 the storm was making it almost impossible to find her front door. Often it happened that the world's water got sucked aloft and came down all at once as rain. She swept her little dog into her arms and felt her way onto the porch. They were both completely drenched, the dog's red coat so wet it looked black. For a while they sat there in the glider, surrounded by thundering curtains of rainwater. 1511MV—what kind of a license plate was that? One plus five plus one plus one equaled eight, a number signifying the World, the very essence of the sorcerer's domain. If you knocked eight on its side it became the symbol of infinity.

As she sat there on the porch she tried getting a sense of what was going on in number 47, the house attached to hers where Mary lived. If she had ever had a daughter the girl would have been like Mary—they even looked a little bit alike, both being bird-boned and pale, and parting their limp mouse-brown hair girlishly down the middle. Miss Vicks's part was always ruler-straight, though, whereas Mary's jogged to the left at the back of her head, suggesting a lack of interest in things she couldn't see. Her teeth were too big for her mouth, too, making her appear more vulnerable than she really was.

Usually in the summer with the windows open Miss Vicks had no trouble eavesdropping on Mary's family, but now the rain was drowning out everything except itself. Could that have been the piano? Her ears often played tricks on her, making voices come from things that couldn't speak, especially machines that had a rhythmic movement like the washer. She'd been feeling uneasy ever since she heard Mary ask where Eddie was and Roy Duffy say he disappeared. Even after the rain had stopped pouring from the sky and dripping from the trees and streaming from the gutter spout—even after the street was restored to silence, the only thing she could hear besides the porch glider squeaking on its rusting joints and the yip her dachshund let out when she made a move to get up was a loud whispering coming from Mary's parents' living room, a sound that always suggested urgency to her and made her feel powerless and left out, cast back into the condition of childhood in a world where the adults were too busy to notice whatever those things were that were tunneling under the streets and slipping from their holes at night to dart under porches and along the telephone wires. Then the bells would start to peal, a stroke for each soul. She gave up and went inside and went to bed.

It was only when everyone on the street was asleep that the robots came flying out of number 37. There were four of them, two the size and shape of needles and two like coins, their exterior surface burnished to such a high state of reflective brilliance that all a human being had to do was look at one of them for a split second to be forever blinded. The robots waited to come out until after the humans were asleep. They'd learned to care about us because they found us touchingly helpless, due in large part to the fact that we could die. Unlike toasters or vacuum cleaners, though, the robots were endowed with minds. In this way they were distant relatives of Body-without-Soul, but the enmity between the sorcerer and the robots ran deep.

IN THE MORNING MISS VICKS HANDED OUT SHEETS OF colored construction paper. The students were to fold the paper in half and in half again and then in half again, the idea being that after unfolding the paper they would end up with eight boxes, in each of which they were to work a problem in long division. Mary filled her boxes with drawings of Eddie, some of them not so bad; arithmetic bored her and besides, it was her plan to be an artist of some kind when she grew up. A feeling attached to the act of being given instructions involving paper and folding it, a feeling of intense apprehension verging on almost insane excitement.

From time to time Mary looked to her left to where her model usually sat. His seat was empty, his yellow pencil lying in the groove at the top of the desk, covered with tooth marks. Eddie chewed on the pencil when he was nervous; he was a high-strung boy, sensitive and easily unhinged. One day last summer Mary had lost control of her bicycle in front of the Darlings' house. She had fallen off and skinned her knee and Eddie stood for a long time staring at the place on the sidewalk where he could see her blood. "I shouldn't have let it happen," he said, even though he'd been at the dentist having a cavity filled at the time.

They were too young, really, to understand the implications, but their bond was of the kind Miss Vicks still hoped for, exquisite and therefore unbreakable, according to the rules governing chemical bonds, in this universe at least.

"Do you know where Eddie is?" Mary asked the teacher when she came around to collect the papers. "Does anyone know where he went?"

"I'm sure he's fine," Miss Vicks replied, even though she wasn't. If Mary's failure to do the assigned work troubled her she kept it to herself.

At recess Cindy XA climbed down from the top of the jungle gym to sit beside Mary on one of the wooden seats of the swing set. "Scooch over," Cindy said, shoving her with her little butt to make room.

Cindy was petite, her bright blonde hair cut very straight, the bangs kept back from her face with red bow-shaped barrettes—Mary didn't like her all that much. They'd tried trading cards throughout the summer but the deals had been oddly unsatisfying. Cindy always gave in without a fight. Being immune to desire, she found the enterprise pointless. As a robot she knew that human bodies had been created to an identical template, one that had been established long ago and owed almost everything to the skeletal structure of the great apes. Apes or humans—we all made the same mistake, tempted by shifting leaves or the smell of sex, by music or a ripe banana. She also knew Miss Vicks didn't have a clue what had happened to Eddie.

"Hang on," Cindy said, linking arms with Mary and pushing off from the playground with her new brown oxfords.

A robot's pressure is slight yet forceful. The swing began to go higher, propelling the two of them back and forth and up and down at a speed so swift as to make Mary increasingly bilious as she watched the iron fence posts blur into a heaving wall of black interrupted by blobs of green and patches of bright blue sky. Eventually she and Cindy were no longer visible.

I think the robot was trying to warn her about what was going to happen.

I think this because the story of what was going to happen is also my story, the story of girls everywhere.

Mary wanted to ask Cindy to make the swing stop but her lips wouldn't move. The trees at the far side of the yard whirled their tresses, shaking all the little birds out, the red ones and the blue ones and the brown ones, and suddenly Mary was alone in the corner of the playground the trash blew into that smelled like cat piss.

When she reached into her pocket she pricked her finger on a pin-like object she hadn't known was there. What is this horrible thing? she wondered. She took it out of her pocket and dropped it to the ground where it lingered briefly before flying back home to its companions.

Number 37

THEIR PORCH WAS IDENTICAL TO MISS VICKS'S ONLY without the glider, but the air around it was different from the air everywhere else, being a little heavier and harder to breathe. It was as if the air around number 37 contained more ions, or the life lived in the house left behind as residue a slight glow that had weight to it, the blue-orange tint of a badly adjusted pilot light. There was a smell, too, impossible to pin down, and even in the dead of night a sound like distant chatter.

Most of us didn't realize what they were when they first moved in. Mrs. Darling took over the same friendship cake she took to all new arrivals, a burdensome gift that came with starter batter and had to be passed on like a chain letter. They were a nice-looking couple, Mr. and Mrs. XA, though Mrs. Darling reported back that even a month after the move their things were still in boxes. The two girls seemed charming, if a little wooden. They had sat on the porch together, the adults drinking martinis and the children apricot nectar; it would never have occurred to you to think they were anything other than people if it weren't for the fact that the mosquitoes were awful that night and Mrs. Darling was the only one they were biting—eating her alive, as she put it, emphasis on *alive*. After the truth came out someone got up a petition to make them move, but it never really amounted to much. By this time there was nowhere they couldn't be found—even in the best neighborhoods.

It was difficult for them, too. One of the worst aspects of the human condition for the robots to accept was the way the things they found around them in number 37, the articles of furniture inside the house, the fabric and paint and the wallpaper—not to mention the objects in the refrigerator—kept falling apart or going bad. Food in particular disgusted them, as did the fact that humans ate it, a sight they had to learn to endure. It was with something approaching horror that they would observe our great mouths creaking open to reveal strands of moistly gleaming saliva and twin rows of white teeth bearing down on a piece of some dead creature's flesh that would burst apart as they watched, releasing streams of juice.

On the other hand, their experience of what happened when the spinnerets of human love threw delicate threads up against and into their receptors, clogging the mechanism, somehow managed to approximate for them the pain of human heartbreak.

As the season changed, night fell earlier and the leaves of the sycamores turned yellow, likewise falling, spangling the sidewalks. The air turned chill. The passage of time made no sense to the robots; their farsightedness extended backward and forward in ways that bore no relationship to it. They could see everything that had happened and everything that was going to happen—the only thing they couldn't do was change what they saw. The robots needed us to change things, the same way we needed them to think for us. Of course what they saw looked completely different.

Miss Vicks, for example—when the sun shone through her dachshund's russet earflaps she experienced deep inside herself a sensation of softness and smoothness that made her feel as though Cupid had shot her through the heart. She had to nip her front teeth together as if she were trying to snip a thread, so overcome was she by feelings of unsurpassed tenderness—she couldn't help herself. Whereas when the robots looked at the earflaps—the *pinnas*, they called them—their tendency was to focus on the physical composition, including the exterior coat of very short fine hair and the pink internal tissue, the brachiating veins, the blue-red membrane. The idea of *soft* remained completely alien to them, yet they began approximating some sense of it through study of Vicks, M.'s face, its composition not unlike the dog's and therefore porous and providing access to the brain, where they watched the thoughts take shape. As a girl she had been fond of a book that began, "And can this be my own world?"

It was a late afternoon in the month of October—the "Column of the Year," as the robots called it, the month's thick, almost substantive yellow light holding the rest of the year aloft above the darkness lapping at its feet. In keeping with her custom, Miss Vicks was walking her dog through the ruined gardens of the Woodard Estate, doing her best to stay on the path, which was hard to see. School had ended for the day and she was tired; the story of Christopher Columbus always presented a challenge, given its less than laudable view of human nature. Every time she taught it, the idea of a band of outsiders taking over a whole continent in exchange for a few "small red caps" struck her as sadder than it had the time before, Columbus's tireless description of steering west through uncharted waters sadder still. "Continuing course west," he wrote in his log, "steering westsouthwest, the seamen terrified and dismayed though no one can say why." What everyone took for land turned out to be a cloud.

The robots flew along behind Miss Vicks like fairies, navigating their way amongst an impenetrable stand of lilac bushes overgrown with stringweed and creeper, keeping their distance so as not to blind her. It was unusual for the robots to be out during daylight hours, but they had been troubled by the sequence of events set in motion by the sorcerer's visit to the street.

The Woodard Estate used to be a brilliant jewel on the brow of the third of the three little green hills you came to upon leaving the schoolyard, after passing the water tower and crossing the old railroad bridge. Before the line got abandoned for being unprofitable, trains used to run there, some of them with dining cars and sleepers and observatories, the profiles in their lit windows suggesting a whole world of human passions and schemes and projected destinations alluringly out of reach. Now the tracks, like the lilacs, were overgrown with stringweed and creeper; deer used them as did the large gray hares that were just beginning to show up everywhere. Neighborhood children continued to ride their bicycles there even though they'd been warned not to, the ties having turned black with rot years earlier.

The first Mr. Woodard bought the land with money he made trafficking in heroin, a fact overshadowed by his widespread and widely publicized philanthropic activity. He designed the mansion himself, a biscuit-yellow Italianate palazzo with real as well as trompe l'oeil balconies and espaliered fruit trees and wall niches containing Greek gods and goddesses, and he was also responsible for the design of the grounds, a network of paths and allées linking fountains hedged round with cedar, sculpture gardens and pergolas, an impossible boxwood labyrinth, and an elaborate system of streams and formal pools all feeding into one large pond with an island in the center surmounted by a "ruin." It was said he'd arranged for his body to be deposited in a freezer in

an underground crypt where it was being held in suspended
animation for the day when humankind would have figured
out once and for all how to cheat death. Or maybe he was
still on the loose somewhere. Miss Vicks's students claimed
the place was haunted.

Nothing looked like what it was here. The stringweed
and creeper covered everything, leaving behind only the general shapes of things, disquieting like the sheeted furniture
in Victorian novels, and what appeared to be paths often
turned out to be trails made by animals or an aboveground
system of drains, so if you weren't careful you would sprain
your ankle in a rabbit hole or pitch into a cistern and drown.
This is why parents warned their children to stay out of the
place. Miss Vicks knew her way around though; she came
here often. It was her intention to take her dog for a walk
and be home before nightfall, which, following the equinox,
came earlier every day.

As she picked her way along a paved path, the surface of
which was crazed and bunched like a tablecloth and laced
with weeds, she heard in the surrounding tangle of shrubbery a faint buzzing that she thought was being made by
flies or bees—I think it's often possible for a person to lie to
herself while at the same time knowing perfectly well what's
going on. The robots' language may have been so foreign as
to sound otherworldly but the mechanism that produced the
speech had a familiar quality, combining the clicking, jet-
like noises of a magnetic resonance imaging machine with
the disconcerting sound of one human's voice issuing from
another human's port. The truth is, Miss Vicks overheard
her name.

Marjorie, Marjorie—it was like a song played on a triangle. The wind began to blow and the air to grow suddenly
cold as if a thin veil of pretense had been let fall, the illusion of light and heat withdrawn, all the planets swimming

closer, drawing into their orbits the dark chill nothing of
outer space. "Is this because the season's changing?" she
asked herself, "or is this the way the world really is, or is
this my mood?" Her little dog, usually eager to plunge on
ahead, had dug in his paws, and she had to tug hard at the
leash to get him to move.

Since the last time Miss Vicks had been to the estate there
seemed to have arisen a beautiful bed of high reeds in place
of the bocce court, beyond which the pond lay diamond-
sown and rippling in the late-afternoon wind. Often in the
past she would rendezvous with the sorcerer on the island in
the pond's center, in the ruin modeled after a dead queen's
temple of love. She would row herself across the water in the
rowboat he left waiting for her in the shallows, a small boat,
its blue paint peeling and the cross thwart cracked down the
middle. As for how he got there himself—she never gave
any thought to that. He could fit his whole hand inside her,
his long fingers cupped like he was about to pluck something out. Maybe he did, for certainly she felt less whole
after he was done.

There was no waiting rowboat today, and the pond seemed
bigger than usual. Something like a large cloud slid into the
sky above Miss Vicks's head and came to a halt. It was too
early for the scows but sometimes you'd see an object up
there you were supposed to ignore.

He had appeared without warning on her street the other
night, driving too fast, interrupting the boys' baseball game.
Like a normal man he considered himself an excellent
driver even though he never paid attention to what he was
doing—he could have hit someone. Miss Vicks always paid
attention; she paid attention to everything. She knew there
hadn't been any reeds here before, but now the bed seemed
to be growing, spreading out on either side and the pond
also to be getting bigger, more like a lake, its far shore no

longer visible and its surface troubled by large gray-green foam-crested waves. Meanwhile the reeds seemed to be getting taller as she stood there, the long blackish pipes of their stems pushing up taller and taller around her, whistling in the wind, their feathery heads breaking apart in her face, releasing clouds of fluffy seeds that got into her eyes and ears and nostrils, and made it increasingly difficult for her to see or hear or breathe.

Her dog was whimpering now as he lay on the ground among the reeds, his soft red coat completely hidden under a shifting blanket of down. Coming to meet her lover Miss Vicks had often had this sense of thwarted will, like when a large insect flies mistakenly into a room through an open window and then keeps flying around and around, attracted to all the wrong things, mirrors or framed photographs, heat registers or—sadder still—a closed window, without ever realizing that all it needs to do is go out the window it came in through and it will be guaranteed a blue sky and a fresh breeze and the prospect of a life that won't be cut short by the angry swat of a rolled newspaper.

"Get up!" she said. The sun was bright red and more ball-like than usual, falling into the place behind the reeds where there used to be a pond. She pushed the stems aside, furious. "Get up!" she said again, as upset by the way she was talking to her dog—her sweet little dog who never did anyone any harm—as she was by everything else. "What am I doing here?" Miss Vicks wondered aloud. "Whose life is this?"

All at once she could see the blue rowboat approaching across the wild gray-green water, its bow rising and falling in the swells.

At first she heard nothing but the plash of the oars, followed by voices, a boy's and a girl's.

"Then what?" the boy was saying. It was hard to hear his voice but Miss Vicks knew it was Eddie—she could barely make out his features in the gathering darkness, his white teeth and thick dark hair.

"Then you're going to have to give it to him, like you promised," the girl said. "Before he has to come after it himself." Fireflies were alighting in a row upon the yellow coil of her hair, after which they turned to diamonds.

"What if I change my mind?" Eddie asked.

"Don't make jokes," the girl replied. "I'll be watching."

"I'm not making a joke," Eddie said.

Miss Vicks couldn't hear the rest. Her dog started to bark and Eddie's voice broke apart into static. Night had fallen; the girl made herself very small and flew into his pocket. A few stars were twinkling around the quarter moon.

Prom Dress

I WISH THIS WAS A DIFFERENT STORY. THE VESSELS sailed and sailed and eventually they fell off the edge. You can have all the information in the world and what good does it do you? The edge of the world is a real place; when you have no soul there are no limits. There was a game everyone used to play at birthday parties called musical chairs. A parent would put a record on the record player and cheerful music would start up, disguising the fact that someone was about to be cast into the outer dark where the fairies live.

Eddie returned to school as if nothing had happened and Miss Vicks acted as if he had never been gone, withholding the favors she usually granted sick students like clapping the erasers or feeding the goldfish. She knew it wasn't Eddie though, that the thing sitting in Eddie's seat wasn't the same Eddie who'd been sitting there before. She couldn't take out a measuring tape and measure him but she felt sure he was bigger—bigger and less apprehensive and nowhere near as sweet. Down came the sailing vessels, up went the turkeys. The first-grade teacher married a man with legs made of wood. It was a mast year; a tremor ran through all the mothers. The wind blew. The clouds spread out and draped themselves across the face of the weather. A snowflake fell and then another and then many snowflakes. There was a holiday recital during which Cindy XA did twenty solo fouettés, passing wraithlike through matter like a neutrino.

The wind was a woe but not personal. Spiky black balls blew off the sycamores lining the street. Two of the "special" children sickened and died. At some point in high school Mary got contact lenses and stopped wearing glasses; Eddie was very tall now and slicked his hair back with a comb he carried in a shirt pocket located in the same place as the one the girl with golden hair had flown into years earlier. There was never any question that he and Mary would become sweethearts, but things never went back to being the way they'd been when they were young.

Even so, the look of Eddie—his obvious preoccupation with a secret he kept hidden from everyone, the way he glanced from under his lowered eyelids while counting something off on his fingers, *one, two, three*—excited Mary; she would sneak out of class to meet him in the last stall in the girls' bathroom. Though he insisted he wasn't any different from the way he'd always been, something about him felt completely different to her, almost like he was made of the same material as the horse they had to jump across in gym. Whenever she tried asking him where he'd gone that summer night so many years ago he looked at her like she was crazy. "Don't be a jerk," he'd say. "I never went anywhere."

But she knew Eddie wasn't telling her the truth. Ever since that night the world had been lit differently—everything had grown brighter, much too bright, really, facing west toward the world's rim.

Of course he was her date for the prom.

The dress Mary wore was on loan from the robots—the master bedroom closet at number 37 contained many such treasures, though, sadly, the original Mrs. Andersen's feet had been a lot smaller than hers. The dress, on the other hand, seemed like it had been made for her. "You have to come try it on after school," Cindy told Mary, the idea being that they were supposed to behave like friends. As far as Mary knew, she was the first person invited inside number 37 since the robots moved to the neighborhood.

The house felt overpoweringly stuffy. The windows were never opened, the robots having no need of air, and the sofa cushions were lumpy and slick, the robots having no need of comfort either. At the time of Mary's visit they were flying around and around the ceiling fixture, making a faint sound like hedge clippers—as soon as she was gone they planned to roost there and recharge. She could hear the sound they made but she didn't know what was making it. She could also hear a muffled set of thumps, exactly like the sound a pair of feet might make coming down a flight of stairs, though she couldn't see anyone. It seemed like the sound was coming from the other side of the wall in number 39, like the way Miss Vicks's feet sounded to her coming down the stairs in number 49, only heavier. The people who lived in number 39 had moved out right after the robots moved in. A For Sale sign appeared on the front lawn, but it got taken down soon afterward.

Presently something came into the room and sat beside Mary on the sofa. Its physical presence was cold and large and animal-like yet not so heavy that it made a dent in the cushion; it had sour breath with a sweet edge as if it had just eaten those pellets the special children in room 12 fed their guinea pig. This must be Downie, Mary thought.

Before the robots moved into the house the Andersens had lived there. Mr. Andersen had been a famous scientist, Mrs. Andersen a housewife, Cindy and Carol their two lovely daughters. Eventually a third child joined the family. They called him Downie because of the extreme softness of his hair; for some reason his lanugo never fell out, leaving him covered with a beautiful coat of soft, grayish hair. Downie was a large, plump boy, sweet and tender like Mrs. Andersen had been, but he could do nothing for himself, which turned out to be a problem the Andersens didn't know how to handle. At some point they must have moved him next door into number 39, though Mary couldn't figure out how he'd managed to get into number 37 without her seeing.

"Mary," Downie said. "You're as pretty as Cindy said."

"Cindy said I was pretty?"

In his lap she could see a bundle of pink fabric that she thought might be the prom dress.

Above her head the robots were going wild. Even though whatever was sitting beside her on the sofa had done nothing to hurt her they knew that if it wanted to it could crack her in two, suck out the meat and throw away the rest, like a person eating a lobster.

"Mary," Downie said. "I can't give this to you until we get a few things straight. No no no! Don't look at me. You can look at me later. Look over there!"

A very old television, one of the ones with a small oval screen in a large wooden box, had come on across the room, but before it did Mary had caught a glimpse of a pair of large sad blue eyes, their blueness swimming around in a wide, open face. There wasn't much to see in the way of programming, mostly a few ancient reruns. "Good work," said a man wearing a white cowboy hat and a white shirt laced up the front like a shoe. This was Sky King and he was commending his niece for handing over to him the stolen ruby she had just found tied to a carrier pigeon's leg. The actor who played the part would die in a car crash on his way to watch the launch of the space shuttle *Challenger*, later sparing him the sight of what became, for its day, a tragedy of epic proportion.

"Mary Mary Mary!"

Mary continued to stare at the TV but nodded her head to let Downie know she was listening.

"We're pinning all our hopes on you," Downie said.

"On me?"

"You've got a big job ahead," Downie said. "You know that, don't you?"

"A big job?"

The room had grown so still Mary could hear only the sound of something inside herself quietly pounding. The volume on the TV was turned all the way down and the robots were lying on the rug in the light cast by the TV screen, glinting like spilled pocket change.

"A lot of time is going to go by, or at least that's what it's going to seem like to you, and the timing is going to have to be just right. More than just right. It's going to have to be perfect. Everything hinges on its being perfect, like the hinge on a door. If the hinge doesn't work perfectly the door is useless. Plus you're not going to get much in the way of advance warning, and by the time you get it you're going to have forgotten we ever had this conversation. You're going to have forgotten a lot of things, including what's at stake. The most important thing to remember is that a duplex's properties are stretchable but they aren't infinite. One minute the opening will be right there in front of you, and the next minute you won't even know where it went. I don't have to tell you that, do I? You live in one yourself. You've heard the way Miss Vicks drops things, the way she bangs the drawers and doors and windows. You've had the contact dreams."

"I'm not sure," Mary said, thinking. It was true that sometimes while she slept all she saw were great shimmering panels of numbers, as sharply bright and beyond reckon as stars in the sky. Other times she felt something lowering itself into her. It would start pumping and it would be like water entering water through a hose, turning her sleek like a seal and without thoughts but a pulse, and when she woke she'd be drenched in sweat.

On the TV screen the little Cessna Sky King called the Songbird took off, carrying him and his niece home to their ranch in Arizona. Mary felt a hand reach for hers and when she looked, there was Cindy sitting on her other side in her cheerleader uniform. Outside the house Miss Vicks's dachshund was barking the high-pitched excited barks that could only mean one thing—the sorcerer was in the neighborhood.

"You have to go home," Cindy said, looking anxiously out the bay window.

"I thought you wanted me to try the dress on first," Mary said.

"There isn't time for that now," Cindy told her.

THE PROM DRESS WAS PINK AND HAD A PRINCESS NECK-line and a full skirt composed of overlapping layers of taffeta and tulle. There was what looked like a small cigarette burn near the hem, practically invisible.

"Smoking must have been fun," Mary said to Eddie.

In keeping with prom night tradition, he had reserved a booth for them at the Captain's Table. The restaurant was filled with other promgoers and chaperones; it had a nautical theme, its walls covered with paintings of seascapes by local artists, not a one of whom had ever been anywhere near the sea.

While Eddie was busy studying the menu, Mary was studying the hem of her dress, trying to avoid having to look at the painting hanging above their booth. In it a sailboat sat directly atop the water in the light of the moon. The water had a curve to it like the meniscus on a glass of milk but otherwise looked rock solid. You could almost *feel* the painter trying to get the water right and failing—"missing the boat," Mary said—though maybe all she was feeling was Eddie's wish for her to stop talking about the painting in such a loud voice.

"I'm going to have the combination plate," Eddie said. "Only without shad. What about you?"

"I hate shad too," Mary said. She thought Eddie looked especially good tonight in his black tuxedo and red baseball cap. Not only had he ended up handsomer than everyone expected, he'd also been elected captain of the baseball team. "Order me the same," she said, holding Mrs. Andersen's purse aloft suggestively. "You know where to find me."

The waiter pointed her down a long hallway, unlit aside from a red bulb flickering at the end of it. Mary proceeded cautiously, the only other source of light the glow from around the door to the kitchen.

Her plan was to wait for Eddie in the bathroom the way she did at school, with her skirt hiked up around her waist and her underpants down around her ankles. At school there was barely enough room in the last stall for him to press her against the wall, and when she tilted her head to kiss him she would see the same spiderweb that had been there since they'd been in seventh grade. Now that they were seniors, usually he was the one who brought the whiskey, but tonight Mary had Mrs. Andersen's flask.

A trickle of music entered the restaurant bathroom through speakers in the ceiling. The room was nicer than the one at school but not much; there were two stalls with dark wood doors and old-style toilets, a pedestal sink just for show, a photograph of a dog wearing sunglasses and a fur stole to hide the dactilo port. "Hi there," Mary said to herself in the mirror. She smiled before she remembered that she couldn't stand the sight of herself smiling. The French twist was a nice touch though, and pink was a good color on her; it made her look young even though she knew she had been endowed with the disposition of an old person long before she actually became one.

Mary went into the stall and pulled down her panties and

waited. They were pink like her dress and embroidered with black flowers. Soon enough someone else entered the bathroom. But Eddie would never wear shoes like the ones Mary saw through the opening at the bottom of her stall door, their pointed tips pausing there in front of her for a moment before turning into the stall next to hers. She heard a zipper being unzipped, the protracted sound of a man urinating, like coins falling into a box on a bus.

"That's better," said the sorcerer.

The proximity of Mary filled him with excitement; he had to work to slow his breathing. A drop, another drop—he was flicking his penis dry. It grew long and thin, the corona pointed and cleft like a hoof. "Don't worry," the sorcerer said. "Your boyfriend's preoccupied." He shifted his feet. "Hello in there. Are you listening to me?"

When she didn't answer he tapped the wall between them once, hard, with the sharp tip of his index fingernail. "You're right—every idiot thinks he can paint water. It takes genius and even then—well, I don't have to tell you."

Mary still didn't answer. A large black ant was walking along the ledge that held the toilet tissue and she made herself focus on it, the way its abdomen was gleaming like patent leather. She had never felt so naked in her life.

"If you were an ant, you wouldn't be stuck in there that way," the sorcerer said, and as he did the ant came to a halt. "Don't cry," he said.

"I'm not crying!" Mary replied, though she hadn't realized she was until he said so.

Meanwhile the sorcerer had what he'd come for; he had taken what he needed to get erect. Now all he had to do was keep the result viable until he could ejaculate it later into a jar. From one receptacle into another—that was the system. He had many such jars that he screwed into lids attached to a ceiling panel in his basement workshop, a system popular among do-it-yourselfers for storing nails of various sizes. But this jar was different; this jar was part of a plan that had come to him in a dream. The sorcerer knew how to sow fear inside human bodies or in their places of habitation, among the folds of their brains or the leaves of their trees; in this way he always got what he wanted. The difference this time was that Mary was his fate. In the dream he saw her face, very close up, including the pores and the small colorless hairs. She was old in the dream and that was the most important part of all, for without the things living and dying on it, what was the world to him except a useless lump of rock?

"How did you know I was crying?" Mary asked, sniffling.

But it was too late; the sorcerer had left the stall.

The dactilo port filled the bathroom with its sudden infusion of brilliant blue-violet light. Mary folded herself over her knees and burst into tears; from her head came the soundless commotion of a port set on vibrate. "MARY! MARY!" said the robots. "MARY! MARY!" It sounded like $@&!!**$$#!!! Mary pulled herself together and returned to the restaurant.

Eddie was sitting exactly as she'd left him, only now there was food on the table in front of him getting cold.

"Why didn't you start without me?" Mary asked. She felt the way she often did after crying, like there wasn't as much of her as there'd been before.

When she took her seat she could feel the sorcerer's body aligned perfectly with her own, back to back, on the other side of the booth, exuding heat through the leather upholstery. If she moved to get away from him he moved too. "Look," she said. "They gave us the shad anyway."

The fish was positioned in the exact middle of her plate next to the sac containing its roe. At three o'clock there was a mound of creamed corn, a corn muffin at six; Mary couldn't recognize the items at nine and twelve. "This isn't what we ordered," she said, pushing the food around with her fork. She made a face. "I waited and waited," she whispered. "It was awful. Did you forget?"

Eddie leaned toward Mary; there was a lewd curl to his lip. "It was *her* doing," he mouthed, pointing. "She was acting really weird."

"How do you mean?"

"Shh," Eddie said. "I don't want *him* to hear. She came over here while you were gone and when the waiter arrived she placed the order but she hadn't even opened the menu. She told me not to worry and when I said, worry about what, she looked at me like I was kidding. She told me everything would be OK in the end."

In the next booth sat the sorcerer's date, Miss Vicks, clad in luminous black satin and coughing as she exhaled a plume of cigarette smoke that arose, tapering from top to bottom like a ghost in the empty darkness above Mary's head. Smoking was against the law but the sorcerer was beyond the law and so by extension was his companion, who looked so little like their old elementary school teacher it was hard to believe her capable of teaching anybody anything. Then again, they'd never seen her on a date before.

"I've heard the band is supposed to be out of this world," Miss Vicks was saying, ashing her barely smoked cigarette in the remains of her dinner.

Mary slid across her seat to the side of the booth nearest the wall, and the sorcerer slid with her.

"What's wrong?" Eddie asked.

"Nothing," Mary said. Her upper lip was moist with perspiration. "Let's ask for the check, shall we?"

"The band, Vicky?" the sorcerer was saying. "Good luck getting *me* on the dance floor."

Later at the prom Mary rested her head on Eddie's shoulder. This was what the girlfriend was supposed to do. She tried to hear his heartbeat through the fabric of his tuxedo jacket, and the fact that she wasn't sure whether she could hear it made her think about how hard it was for any girl to ever know whether her love was being returned. The gymnasium had been transformed, showers of tiny colored lights completely masking the dark wood walls and the scuffed hardwood floor and the narrow balcony that circled the upper level where Eddie and his fellow athletes ran laps in inclement weather and where the chaperones were now passing around a bottle of vodka.

The theme was the Rain of Beads, which some teachers had objected to as inappropriate, but their objections had been overridden by the prom committee. If it wasn't possible to reinvent the past in such a way as to make it conform to the present's cheerful view of the way things ought to have been, why bother living? Red lights for blood and yellow for plasma and blue for tears—human beings needed to be proud they were made of such things!

Couples twirled snowflake-like past Mary and Eddie, who were barely moving. No one's gown was as perfect as hers, not even the prom queen's. A photographer snapped several shots for the local newspaper, capturing the pair from behind, a few of Mary's moist brown locks escaping the upsweep of her do, the fingers of Eddie's one hand tight around her waist and the other outspread across her shoulder blades. Everyone had seen Eddie fly sideways above center field with that same hand outspread, the ball nesting in his glove like an egg. He had been scouted by the major leagues—unlike most of his classmates, Eddie had a future.

The king and queen of the prom presided over the affair from their separate thrones, holding hands. These were Roy Duffy and Cindy XA—the vote hadn't even been close. Who handsomer than Roy in his beaded tux, who prettier than Cindy in her matching gown? Would the king and queen have sex following the dance like most of the other couples? They'd been seen kissing in the field parking lot after baseball practice. Roy's knuckleball was all but un-hittable; Cindy could assume positions the other cheerleaders only dreamed of.

The irony was not lost on any of us that despite the theme there was a robot on the throne.

The Rain of Beads

T HE STORY OF THE RAIN OF BEADS GOES BACK FAR enough to seem like it never really happened. The girl I first heard it from was always telling stories—she was one of the older girls and all the little girls were in awe of her. We were sitting on the porch stoop one night in late summer, trading cards. This was what you did if you were a girl— it was your calling. The cards were separated into packs according to category: still lives, famous paintings, horses, dogs. Most of the trading cards had been bought in a store and had an unpleasant texture that made them less desirable than the jokers stolen from the decks of cards everyone's parents used for bridge or poker. These playing cards were larger and smoother to the touch and often came in pairs. The girl wanted a black horse to complete the pair with her white horse. Her name was Janice.

Generally speaking the adults on the block considered her a liar. She said her mother beat her with a willow branch and she had stripes on her back to prove it. She said humans had been right when they said the world was flat and round like a coin and you could fall off the edge. Many things everyone had been told weren't real turned out to be real. The world had edges but you couldn't see them going, only when you were trying to come back. Janice also said she had a brother who died of leukemia and that, amazingly enough, turned out to be true. Like everyone else, she could push buttons on a console and find out whatever she wanted to know about anybody or anything. For this reason she kept everything exceptional about herself hidden.

Janice's parents were at work all day long. She was their only living child and they loved her dearly, though the older she got the harder it was for them to show it. Her mother worked in a lab at the university; her father sold the other fathers clothing. The newlyweds in the house that was the other half of theirs were paid to keep an eye on her when she got home from school, but the whole street knew they spent every waking hour in bed. If she got lonely she had the family pet for company. She taught the dog to balance a cracker on his nose until she said OK, and then he'd dip his head and let the cracker drop to the floor and then he'd eat it.

The afternoons had a way of stretching endlessly in all directions as if time were taffy, something a person could get caught in. Janice said time was different now. It used to be sadder. The couple next door fought to get themselves in the mood. They would scream at one another and then Janice could hear the bedsprings creaking through the wall behind her parents' headboard.

Once there was a girl, Janice said. Like most girls, she was a sap. By now everyone was listening, even the girls who were pretending not to.

In the beginning the fair tree of the Void abounded with flowers, Janice said, acts of compassion of many kinds. The fair tree of the Void also lacked compassion. The two trees sprang from one seed—think of it like code, she suggested— and for that reason there was but one fruit. The girl in the story spent a lot of time, like most girls, wishing for love. If she could have been cut open the boy she had a crush on would have been able to see her inner markings, even though they were practically invisible, like the black dots inside a banana. As it was he never had a chance.

He was a nice person but for some reason he thought it would be funny to pass the girl a note asking her to meet him at the Woodard mansion after school. He lived one block over, Janice said, above the movie theater; he probably got the idea to send the note from some friend. The theater was a family business and that's why to this day they never showed funny movies.

After she returned home the girl washed the breakfast dishes. She stood there with her head bowed, crying into the sink, leaving the nape of her neck exposed all the way through the many different layers of her house and the debris floating in the upper atmosphere to the X-ray vision of the operational apparatus of the scow hovering in the air above.

Think of them like gods, Janice said, because that's what they are. The nape of a human neck is especially easy to see through—that's why they love it when we bow our heads. It doesn't have anything to do with praying. Prayers bore them.

Unlike the boy she had a crush on the apparatus could see through the girl perfectly; it knew it wasn't meant for her but that didn't stop it. It was her fate, which had nothing to do with love. It had nothing to do with the boy and the note, either. Things just worked out this way sometimes.

Janice leaned in close; her attention to personal hygiene left a lot to be desired, and her breath was often stale. Everyone knew she'd stolen the fair tree of the Void somewhere, since her vocabulary wasn't normally that impressive.

Do you know why the girl was crying? Janice asked. She was crying because she felt sorry for the world and everyone in it. The world was sadder then, too, and she wanted everyone to be happy like she was, meeting the boy. If she hadn't wanted that, things would be different now, though not the way she hoped. After she dried the dishes the girl put on her jacket and got on her bike and started out, even though she'd promised her mother and father she wouldn't go anywhere before they arrived home from work. The bike was a red Schwinn with a bell and a basket over the handlebars, sort of like the bike Mary used to have before she married the sorcerer and moved to town.

It was the time of day when the moon and sun are both out at once. The girl rode to the end of the block, across the vacant lot and up the hill past the school and the water tower and over the trestle bridge. The shadow of the scow rode behind her, tapping her onward like a cat toying with the mouse it's about to eat. She loved pumping her legs, feeling her heart beating—from above it was the size of the end of a pencil. The street ran along the western edge of the Woodard Estate and the only way in was a driveway so overgrown with vines she would have ridden right past it if it weren't for the two goddesses crouched atop pillars at the entryway. "Young lady!" Aphrodite called. "Over here!" She was missing her nose, but Athena was missing her whole head, which was a pity since what the girl needed to hear more than anything at this point was the voice of reason.

I'm not telling her name, Janice said, so don't bother to ask. It would make it hard to pay attention to the story.

At first the driveway was almost impassable, and the girl had to get down off her bike to wheel it in. She could see little eyes suspended in the thicket of bushes on either side of her, could hear the sound of small things moving under the blanket of vines, but she was too excited to feel frightened. The light was behaving the way it always did at the end of the day, the sun having hit bottom like an apple thrown down a well. Perhaps this is why she didn't notice when the driveway began to change before her very eyes.

Now the lamps went on, guiding her footsteps. Mechanical things are able to communicate with one another, the way mushrooms grow out of a single long strand of fungus underground. The road was clear of brush and laid with paving stones and up ahead she could see the mansion, the windows brightly lit.

Very eyes, someone said. What are very eyes?

Shh! said someone else.

Inside the mansion the scow's operational apparatus was waiting for her. The system was much less sophisticated in those days. It was a young man, but everything was not quite right about him. Still, it was extremely handsome, in an overly polished, highly buffed way. It could dance, like most robots, better than humans, and the girl was clumsy on her feet. Her father said she could trip on a smooth linoleum floor. She knew right away she'd been tricked, but she didn't mind, because it was giving her its special pleading look, the one it had been designed to give her, to win her heart. It had nothing to do with love! It was her fate, remember? It could come from out of nowhere and mow a person down just like sickness, and no matter how many things the doctors did to try to stop it, no matter how many machines they brought in or how many parts of the sick person's body they replaced with parts of a healthy person's body, it kept moving, killing everything in its path, until all that was left was a jar of ashes.

She was a nice middle-class girl and he was a garbage man, which is the way this often happened in movies. And then he would turn out to be a prince or something like that.

They danced and they danced; the robot knew exactly how to lead the girl to make it seem like she knew what she was doing, and the music helped as well, because it was coming from a peardrum. Next time, he said, bring your friends. He encouraged her to imagine herself whirling among them, the most graceful and beautiful one in the bunch, stirring their envy, because after all she deserved to be envied, he said, just look at you!

It was then she noticed the mirror that ran along the entire side of the ballroom. How can that be, she thought, for the windowpanes reflected in it were missing or broken, with pieces of glass still stuck in the frames like knives, and the outside of the building was overgrown with a thick net of creeper that kept the whole thing from falling in a heap. The dancing partner looked handsomer than ever, the girl herself like a fluid shapeless sac of parts held together by skin and the skin pulsing with blood and pink with smudges here and there of hair and blowing panels of fabric. Meanwhile the creeper was filling with more and more gray-brown birds, hundreds of tiny bright eyes and beaks, cheeping and fluffing their wings.

This was the way robots viewed living flesh ever since they'd been granted the gift of color-sightedness and prophecy to compensate for the fact that they would never know love. In the robot universe there were six windows through which the sun rose, six windows through which the sun set, and the stars moved around opening and shutting the windows like servants. Even though they had no interest in the way humans measured time or how the planets affected their actions, the robots knew Mercury retrograde was a point of crisis for them, inaugurating a period of voluptuous activity, one that would grow more and more intense as the days grew shorter.

Really, it told her. Bring your friends! It told her there was a nice surprise in store for her if she did.

When the girl got home her shoes were torn to ribbons. Her father sat there in his easy chair in his white shirt and khaki pants, looking through his reading glasses at her worn-out shoes, the expression on his face like that of a person going through a closet trying to find some worthless article of clothing he suddenly realized he wanted more than anything. His hair had turned gray at the temples but was otherwise thick and black, his skin mostly unwrinkled. He hadn't changed that much since when he was a boy, really—the girl was the one who had changed. I'm not made of money, you know, her father said and the girl laughed, because who *was?* People weren't made of paper or metal. That was what made them people.

The next day she returned to the mansion, only this time she took her friends. Girls can talk other girls into doing things with them by making it seem like it's the "in" thing to do, like trading cards or taking ballet lessons or going all the way or entering a religious order. When Eddie signed with the Rockets it wasn't because he would have felt left out if he didn't. He loved to play baseball—boys have always been more blatantly competitive and they enjoy roughhousing. Still, for the girl to get her friends to go with her she had to twist the truth. Another thing girls do is lie to get what they want. For instance she didn't mention the mirror or that there was only the one dance partner.

How many friends did she take? someone asked. Because I think I know this story.

Lots, Janice said. Maybe sixteen or seventeen. Twenty? All the girls from her class, anyway. It was the first generation of girls.

That's not the way the story goes, someone else said. There should be *twelve.*

But Janice wasn't telling "The Twelve Dancing Princesses." That was make-believe. This was history.

The girls got to the mansion just as it was getting dark. Like now, Janice said, only night was sadder then. The wind was blowing and it was starting to rain, real rain, not what came later. O western wind when wilt thou blow that the small rain down can rain. Poets used to write things like that. The mansion windows were ablaze and the girls could hear music, very sweet and exciting, strings and horns and woodwinds and maybe, just maybe, if only they'd been listening more closely, if only they'd stopped their endless chatter and paid attention for a change, they also might have heard the *tap-a-tap-tap* of the peardrum.

A peardrum, in case you don't know, Janice said, is shaped like a guitar and has three strings, but only two pegs to tune them with, and a little square box attached to the side for keeping fairies. They're the most beautiful fairies of all; their faces are like crystal but alive, with real eyes that can see and the sweetest little tongues! You never want to let them out, though. They have no regard for human life.

Of course there were enough dance partners to go around— one of the beauties of the operational apparatus was that it could be reproduced infinitely and at the drop of a hat. Every girl thought her partner was the handsomest and that she was the loveliest girl in the room. The later it got the harder it was to hear a thing over the noise of the orchestra and the dancers' feet and the wind and the rain and the gray-brown birds. The girls were never able to compare notes to figure out what was happening—dictators gather crowds for the same reason. The rain swept in through the broken windows. The wind blew away the girls' dresses. They were too busy thinking how ugly all the other girls looked to look at themselves in the mirror.

No one noticed when the first girl got taken up.

Taken up where? someone asked.

I would have noticed, said someone else.

Janice whirled around. You don't notice anything, she said. None of you do! She pointed at the cigar box in my lap. It was empty. Did you see her stealing your cards? she asked. They're your ticket out of here! Don't you know anything? Where are your mothers and fathers? Shouldn't they be calling you in right about now?

It is true, the full moon had risen so high in the sky it didn't look any bigger than the baseball one of the boys had left lying on the grass verge below the stoop. The boys had gone home long ago; the street was perfectly quiet except for the sound of piano music coming from down the block. Whatever it was it was being played at the correct tempo, so it couldn't be Mary.

If I could only begin to be a queen, Janice said, talking to herself, I could go wherever I pleased. She sighed and patted her hair, adjusting her hairdo the way the mothers did.

They were taken up in the scow, she said. One after another. The operator got there first and was treating his girl to a cocktail in a crystal goblet. From above, the mansion looked like a snack cake, with shadows sticking out at angles that didn't make any sense unless you took into account the blue light cast by the scow.

Inside the scow everyone was busy drinking cocktails and trading cards. The robots thought of this as foreplay, having no understanding of physical intimacy. According to the prophecy a child was going to come along that would be part human and part robot and this child was going to change everything. Of course it was way too soon—both sides were totally unprepared, not to mention the fact that they had their parts mixed up. The girls were only interested in romance, and the robots in completing a transaction. Oddly enough, both sides were hoping for the same pair of cards, Blue Boy and Pinkie. The cards originally came from a deck belonging to the girl's parents. Her parents had no need for jokers, since they played bridge, not poker. The cards were beautiful, with gold rims.

I've heard of them, someone said. Those cards were even more beautiful than the horses.

There used to be lots of beautiful cards, said someone else. Then the fairies got loose.

Listen to me, Janice said. Leave the fairies out of this. Do you hear?

Pinkie had belonged to Mary, she said. Everyone knew the story of how the sight of her blood on the sidewalk had moved Eddie to tears. The stain was still there—you just had to know where to look for it. Mary used to think of Eddie as Blue Boy, with his dark hair and soft lips and studiously downcast expression. She thought of Pinkie as herself, even though she would never have dreamed of wearing a hat that had to be tied with pink ribbons. To see her now you'd never know she'd been one of the ugly girls.

There's no such thing as an ugly girl, someone said. My mom told me.

No one bothered to disagree, the idea was so stupid.

At first they didn't notice, they were too busy trading, Janice said. Ever since the wind blew their dresses away the girls were just in their underwear; most of them had on bras, even if they didn't need them. The robots moved closer.

The girl had gotten a little drunk from the cocktail. She was sitting on the floor of the scow when her dance partner reached across the cards piled between her spread legs and slid his finger up under the crotch of her panties. It was cool, his finger, being made of titanium, and he used it to stroke her, first on the outside, running it over her pubic hair until she began to moan, and then sliding it inside her. She'd done this to herself but she'd never had it done to her.

Everyone knows what I'm talking about, right? said Janice. Once you start you can't stop, isn't that so? Just try stopping and see where it gets you.

Now all the girls were lying on the floor with their knees pointing to the ceiling and their legs spread. Everything was going fine as long as the robots kept using their fingers. Give me the card, said the girl's dance partner. The robots had based their plan on information they'd read in a book somewhere: "Rooted fast she'll turn to flame and change her form but keep her love the same."

Give me the card, the girl's dance partner said again, sliding his finger in deeper. The card, or I'll stop. There was one big pile with all sorts of cards in it. There was a fruit basket, a parrot in a cage, a red rose, a white rose, a bridge over a river, a black Lab, a golden Lab, the Mona Lisa, a kitten, a tree, another bridge, a robin, a pear, the Potato Eaters. All of this was being offered for Pinkie. To make the pair with Blue Boy, who was being kept hidden away in the drinks cabinet.

Take it, the girl said. The robot took this to mean the transaction was complete. It lowered itself into her.

What happened next was too horrible to describe. Naturally the girl hadn't changed form the way the robot thought she would—none of the girls had changed form. The information the robots based their plan on was poetry, which they are incapable of understanding.

Janice poked me hard between the ribs.

You think that hurts? she said when I began to cry. That's nothing compared to what it felt like. Nothing. You can't even begin to imagine. Supposedly the sound the girls made was so loud no one could sleep. It wasn't like being torn to pieces, because pieces are big. It was like having the smallest parts of your body like the corpuscles and peptides and nuclei and follicles rip loose from one another, every single one of them. The parts were so small they were practically invisible and all different colors, the main ones being red and yellow and blue. They were gorgeous if you didn't know what they were. There was nothing left of the girls. Nothing for the doctors to replace with new parts, nothing.

The robots washed everything down the drain in the floor of the scow and for days afterward it rained beads. People tried leaving out bowls and buckets and trash cans to catch the parts—there was a rumor that if you caught all the parts of a girl she could be put back together again and you could keep her for your own. The mothers and the fathers tried hardest, of course.

Like Humpty Dumpty, said the littlest girl.

What about the fairies? someone else asked.

Shh, someone said, checking to see if Janice was going to get angry.

But she was off on another planet as she often was after telling a story. It had grown so dark you couldn't see the expression on her face. The lightning bugs were out and they were the only bright thing on the block, except for the light at the other end of the street in Mrs. Trimble's attic, where her grown-up son lay smoking cigarettes and reading books by French intellectuals.

The fairies? Janice said. Look! There's one! She reached out and caught a lightning bug and squashed it in her hand.

You're blaming the robots, right? That's what everyone did. The robots didn't mean to start trouble. They weren't happy about what happened. It was a mistake, and they don't like it when they make mistakes. It was no different from when a nuclear reactor blows up and for years afterward radioactivity rains down from the sky making people sick. It was better than that, even, because the robots wanted to make things better. It wasn't their fault they didn't understand the poem.

That's not a fairy, someone said.

How do you know? Janice sniffed as if maybe she'd been crying, too. No one understands poetry. Another lightning bug flew past and she reached out and caught it. Some things are real and some things are *like* real. The girls died. They died for love. She opened her hand and let the bug go. Everyone watched it drift away across the street until it was too small to see.

The mothers and fathers, though, Janice said. They never got over it. They had to harden their hearts so they wouldn't keep breaking.

You can sit out here forever, Janice said. They're not going to call you in.

Yellow Bear

HIS NAME WAS WALTER WOODARD, THE ELDEST OF the three Woodard boys—Sorcerer was only the most well known of Walter's nicknames. No one could believe it when Mary agreed to marry him. Of course everyone thought she was going to marry Eddie. To imagine one of them without the other was like seeing the sky without the sun in it, an affront to nature, a rift in the fabric of the common good, an invitation to obscenity. Along with the family business—a variety of dark ventures comingling in a sack called "real estate"—the Woodard boys were known to have inherited their father's questionable character, his ability to perform such sleights-of-hand as could turn abomination to gold.

Marriage proved to be a surprise to Mary, who had thought being a wife would mean being constantly busy. Her new neighborhood was quiet, the house all by itself at the end of a long driveway bordered on both sides by rosebushes and backed by a woodlot. They had bought the property to escape the noise of the city, especially the din of people and objects being moved from place to place. It was a lovely house, quite expensive, the walls white as snow inside as well as out. Through every window Mary had a view of growing things driving their shadows deep into the wide suburban lawn.

Her husband claimed the noise of the city had been the source of Mary's problem. Her unhappiness troubled him, as if she were being unhappy on purpose to make a point. When she woke at night from bad dreams he told her she needed to take it easy during the day—nightmares were caused by stress. When she said the dreams weren't her dreams he gave her the look that eventually won her heart. It was exactly like the look Eddie used to give her, one that had been designed to show his fondness for how adorable Mary was, which these days, as far as she could tell, was not very. In a contact dream the dreamer's mind got swallowed by the mind of another dreamer, usually someone who lived in close proximity though not in the same house; this phenomenon occurred most often in the very young or the mentally ill, whose brains lacked such walls as the mature brain erected over time, brick after brick of old passwords, the secret location of a soul, schoolmates' birthdays, how to sew a dress, recognize a prime number. People living in duplexes were especially susceptible, which was why the sorcerer had bought such an isolated house in the first place.

He would lie in bed facing Mary, his face inches from hers, cupping her ears in his hands. How was she expected to hear? If she wanted to get pregnant again, it seemed like he was saying, this certainly wasn't the way. Her life was supposed to be perfect now that all the unpleasantness with the boy was behind her. They never talked about Eddie, the way he brought her home from the prom and that was the last she saw of him. The sorcerer knew the subject was one better left alone.

"I'm not ready for this," Eddie had said to her that night, though Mary later realized that she'd never been exactly clear on what he meant by "this." They were standing under the porch lamp like people in a show, with the Darlings and Miss Vicks in rapt attendance. Eddie didn't want a baby,.

that much was obvious. He'd have to be some kind of an idiot to have a baby now, he told her, just when his career was getting off the ground. It wasn't fair to her, either, he added, though with much less conviction. There was a place she could go—he'd heard about it from one of the fellows he'd be playing with in the fall. Saint Something-or-other, run by nuns; he could get the name from his new teammate. The place was supposed to be nice, not far from the shore everyone on the street used to go to on vacation, and afterward the baby would be adopted by some nice people who couldn't have babies of their own. Better yet, she could just get rid of it. Roy's father was a doctor and he said he'd help out. He would lose his license if she ever told a soul. "You don't have to worry about money, though," Eddie told her. Now that he'd signed with the Rockets, money was the least of their problems.

It wasn't as if Mary wanted a baby. It wasn't even as if she wanted to get married. Everyone kept telling her she had her whole life ahead of her—whatever that meant. No, it was more like a part of her life got sliced into and lifted out like a serving of sheet cake. As it transpired, the nuns were silent and surprisingly lacking in judgment. Sea breezes blew through all the windows of the convent day and night, moving Mary's thoughts around to make unreadable patterns like the grains of sand on the floor of her room.

Meanwhile Eddie disappeared completely after signing with the Rockets. The only way Mary knew he was alive was through Downie, who'd gotten a job at the ballpark as the team mascot. He didn't even need to wear a costume. The sweet summer days turned to star-patched evenings, the ballpark filling with noise and the smell of beer and popcorn. When Downie came to visit he would bring her news of Eddie, but only if Mary asked, and even then it was like pulling teeth.

When she finally returned to the street no one recognized her. She took to bleaching her hair and putting it up in a beehive, wearing large round sunglasses and stiletto heels. Often she could be seen standing with her hips thrust forward, paging through fashion magazines at Resnick's Drugstore. The store still smelled like the horror comics she used to buy back when she first learned to read. She would hand Mr. Resnick her allowance money and carry the comic to the booth farthest from the door so no one would disturb her while she studied the monsters, their misshapen limbs and faces with pieces missing, their fangs and claws and fur and bandages coming undone. The monsters used to make her feel lonely and tenderhearted, unlike the fashion models, who made her feel like a monster. She remembered folding construction paper in Miss Vicks's classroom prior to recess. No one knew where Eddie was then, either. Outdoors hadn't been any better. The drinking fountain water in the bubbler tasted awful. You couldn't see the sun itself, only a flat pan of sunlight on the rough playground floor.

"I wouldn't worry," Miss Vicks told Mary's mother, who in fact didn't. It was Miss Vicks who worried; Mary's mother was too busy thinking about her next drink to worry about her daughter. "Once she gets to art school she'll be herself again," Miss Vicks reassured her.

"Mary's a big girl, Marjorie," said Mary's mother. "She can take care of herself."

Neither woman knew what went on in art school—if she had, she wouldn't have been so sanguine about Mary's prospects. During the day the students were a hive of industry, drawing plaster casts, painting from the model, learning the rules of perspective, stretching canvas. But night was a different story. At night the square they had crossed in the morning to enter the building was transformed, the central fountain no longer a cheerful sunlit place where young mothers came to sit with their baby carriages, gossiping and eating lunch and blocking everyone's view of Aphrodite. At night the fountain became a shrine, the goddess standing there fully revealed in the middle of the water, her body white and naked, her back arched and her breasts lifted to the moon. Elm trees lined the square, their leaves falling ceaselessly through the dark like coins. This is how Zeus got women pregnant.

Mary had to struggle to keep the large canvas she gripped in both hands from catching the wind like a sail and carrying her off.

"Where are you going?" called the blond boy from Cast Drawing. They'd been assigned to the same small room that morning together with an immense Roman head, both of them reduced to helpless laughter by the bust's egglike eyeballs.

"Home," Mary told him, "to work," and he told her she was crazy.

"The Latvians are having a party," he said. "No one does homework in art school."

The question of genius came up during the day but at night it didn't matter. Often at night Mary would find herself in the bed of someone whose paintings she couldn't bring herself to look at by day. Everyone got drunk or high at the parties; the apartments were small and poorly heated and you could hear living creatures walking around in the walls. One boy was a pointillist, meaning when she agreed to pose for him in the nude it took forever. The blond boy only did paintings of rabbits, the big gray hares that were everywhere now, pale-eyed and serious, appearing in the middle of the city streets reared up on their hindquarters as if automobiles posed no threat, though you could see their dead bodies everywhere. "They have gray eyes like you," the boy told Mary, as if she should feel complimented to have her eyes compared to a rabbit's. Eddie used to say her eyes were silver.

After they moved into the new house, Walter insisted on hanging one of Mary's paintings on the living room wall above the sectional sofa, even though she asked him not to. He thought she was being falsely modest, but the painting reminded Mary of a time in her life she'd rather forget. The painting was divided horizontally in three layers and represented the tripartite universe. It was inspired by the work of a Spanish monk who'd lived during the waning years of the first millennium when everyone thought the world was going to end.

The bottom layer was the color of copper, streaked with verdigris and violet, giving it a watery, immaterial look. It was the prettiest layer, even though it stood for the underworld, the bodies of the Aquanauts drifting through it like goldfish. Mary used the same gold leaf on them that she used for stars in the eggplant-colored top layer, neither fish nor stars having any moving parts. The gold leaf shone but enclosed anything it touched in a hard shell—the Spanish monk had used it for halos. If you looked closely you could see fine gold threads linking the stars and the Aquanauts, so thin they were almost invisible, passing through the red middle layer that represented life on earth. The threads tangled around the limbs of regular people trying to get their job done.

"What are these supposed to be?" her teacher asked Mary during a critique. "Air hoses," Mary said, and he sighed and patted her on the head. He was old and often cruel; one time he threw a boy's painting of a poinsettia plant out the window. He was always nice to the girls though, despite the fact that he never nominated them for any of the prizes, the good ones where you got to travel to a foreign country.

The subject of the painting was the Descent of the Aquanauts, a fact Mary had kept to herself until the day not long after they'd moved into the new house when Walter was putting something away in the cellar and found her paintings where she'd hidden them behind the hot water heater. She used to think there would be a greater sense of forward movement in her life, but now it seemed like where a person ended up was going to turn out to have everything to do with where she started.

"That's what I went as to the masked ball," she reminded Walter, as if he would ever forget. "An Aquanaut."

Each October the art school put on a masked ball that was the talk of the town, attended by bohemians and socialites alike. Even the less talented students were good at making costumes, but the costumes the talented students made could take your breath away. One boy was an anamorphic blur that only became himself when you looked at him from the right angle. One girl opened like a Cornell box and a ghost flew out. There were two Brides Stripped Bare, two Saint Francises receiving stigmata, any number of Madame Xs, Winged Victories, sunflowers. The pointillist boy was a trick of light, a mirage. No one would go anywhere near him.

"You should be more careful," her future husband had told Mary, leading her off the dance floor to the upstairs gallery where the drinks were being served. She couldn't dance and the flippers didn't help—to make matters worse she was hallucinating on mushrooms. When he introduced himself to her as Walter Woodard, she laughed. "I thought you were dead," she said, and he told her she was thinking of his father.

Walter was wearing gold hoop earrings and dark glasses, a gold crown and a fuschia tunic with black leggings that showed off his long sleek legs. He fit right into the gallery, with its Moorish jewel-box arches. When Mary asked him what he was supposed to be, he said a sorcerer.

"Can't you tell?" he said. "I can tell what *you* are." Then he leaned down and put his lips to her ear. "You should leave the past alone," he whispered. "Not everybody's going to get the joke."

"I'm not joking," Mary said. She stood there leaning up against him in her black nylon bathing suit with its little black skirt and her white rubber bathing cap, looking up at him through her goggles, her air hose regally draped across the crook of one arm like a train.

"I worry about you," Walter said, and he meant what he said.

Later he followed her into the bathroom and held her shoulders gently as she threw up into the toilet. Then he wet a paper towel with cold water and pressed it to her forehead. "Weren't we in some bathroom together before?" Mary asked, and Walter reminded her she was tripping. "No!" Mary said. "I remember!" He helped her to her feet and took her back to his apartment, which was immense and lavish and looked out over the river. All night long the channel buoys tolled their bells as the big ships slid past them in the darkness.

"IT'S TOO BAD THINGS CAN'T STAY LIKE THIS FOREVER," Walter said to Mary in the morning. They were lying in bed looking up at the ceiling, watching the light cast there by the river as it swam above them, a shifting net of many colors.

"Why can't they?" Mary asked. Of course she thought she knew the answer—the light on the ceiling looked to her like it was being processed by an enormous mind and then filtered through an eye that despite the precautionary veils couldn't bear to see her lying there one second longer. "I feel like I've always known you," she said, clutching at straws, but as she said it she knew it was true. Walter felt familiar to her, beloved even. The truth is, he felt like Eddie, and why shouldn't he?

"Oh, Mary," he said. He took her in his arms and kissed her on the mouth. "It doesn't work that way. You can't always have known me—you know that, don't you? It isn't time that folds, it's space. Didn't you learn all this in school?" Walter was a good kisser—better than Eddie had ever been. "That teacher of yours, didn't she teach you anything?"

"Are you talking about Space Drift?" Mary asked.

She thought she was making a joke like the one she'd made earlier at the masked ball, but Walter gave her a sharp look. "Don't joke about things you don't know anything about," he said.

The next thing she knew they were married.

NOW MARY SAT AT HER SEWING MACHINE GUIDING MATE-rial the exact pink of her prom dress ahead and to either side of the presser foot; as usual it felt like the machine was coming flying at her. The machine had been a wedding present from Downie. It was black with a gold design on its base; when she pressed the pedal the sound the machine made blocked out everything the way the crickets did: *chchch chchchch chhhh.*

The wedding had been a private affair in the Woodard family chapel; at the exact moment Walter slipped the ring onto Mary's finger she'd been surprised to look up and see Downie standing outside the door, holding the large box that turned out to contain Mrs. Andersen's sewing machine. Afterward, when she asked him how he'd known she was getting married, he told her he had his ways. "What do you mean?" Mary asked, and he pointed into the woods. The day was ending; shadows darted between the trunks of the fir trees. It was no secret that in recent years the estate had become overrun with wild animals, the gray hares chief among them. Mary had to clear away their nests and droppings before the ceremony could begin. "They do whatever I ask," Downie said, calling one to him with a little whistle and petting it between its long gray ears. "Just don't get too close. They know how to bite." Later on he gave her Mrs. Andersen's dress dummy too, but as Mary had grown older she'd never developed breasts as large as Mrs. Andersen's had been. Eventually the dummy ended up in the basement along with her paintings.

The dummy reminded Mary of the time before art school when she was living in number 47 with her parents. She thought of her father asleep on the couch, her mother watching him silent and impenetrable, waiting to accommodate him—to accommodate anyone—like the dummy. Mary's parents had to have moved to the street from somewhere else at some point, though Mary was pretty sure she'd never lived anywhere until then except inside her mother. Before that she was nothing, or something that had nothing to do with her, a wasp caught in a curtain. She could hear the sound of buzzing and she could see a face close to hers, staring. Mary couldn't remember what it reminded her of, but she knew it reminded her of something from so long ago it had to have been before she lived in her mother. A wall of snow slid from the roof and landed with a thump like someone had thrown down a dead body. It was night, it was day. She drew back the branches and looked though the opening. The sun crept up the pane of the sky and then summer came. Eddie gave her a kiss.

They were sitting on the damp cement at the bottom of the steps outside her cellar door. Honeysuckle bushes that grew above them blocked the light; a large black ant crawled off the cement onto her foot. Eddie asked Mary if she would show him her underpants and she did, but that was all. They

were white cotton, like all of her underpants. She showed
him how to get the drop of honey out of the honeysuckle
by pulling off the flower. They couldn't have been more
than five.

From where she sat sewing, Mary could see the copper-
colored watery bottom layer of her painting, as well as the
black antlike gleam of the baby grand piano Walter had
given her for their anniversary. "Oh, dear. Oh, Mary," he
said when she burst into tears. "You used to play. Oh, Mary,
I'm so sorry."

The pink material was for the maternity blouse she was
making—not for herself but for Cindy XA, who had come
by one afternoon last week to tell Mary she was pregnant.
Cindy had been wearing a sheath sundress that showed off
what celebrities called their "bump." She was still with Roy
Duffy and had taken his last name even though they'd
never bothered to get married; the Duffys had a nice house
near the ball field where Roy coached the high school
baseball team. Mary knew his baby wasn't growing inside
Cindy; the appliance being used was related to the one Mrs.
Darling had observed the robots use for eating and drinking, a sophisticated compartment that was able to transform
matter like milk or sperm or crackers into electrical energy.
Roy had to know the baby would look nothing like him.
Most babies produced this way started out looking like hand
grenades and were just as likely to explode.

Walter didn't eat much but, unlike the robots, he did eat,
and he had nothing but praise for Mary's cooking. Every
morning he drove off to work in the same silver-gray car that
had appeared on Mary's street when she was a girl. Where
did he go? The world kept him busy. Some days to the water
tower where he took care of paperwork, which for some reason he had a lot of, some days farther than that. Some days
he went back to the street where he first saw Mary. He had

unfinished business there. Usually he came home in the early evening for dinner.

It was summer, golden summer, the roses in full bloom, the pieces of sky Mary could see through the trunks and limbs and lightly trembling leaves of the trees outside the windows blue like lapis lazuli. When a person wore it as an adornment it signified truthfulness, but in a sky it signified nothing. A little breeze, the smell of grass, a few bugs, that was it. She held up the blouse and regarded her handiwork. It could certainly use something more, some white rickrack around the hem. *She* could use something more. Something along the lines of some beautiful golden whiskey in a small, clear glass. She and Eddie used to have the best time together, drinking whiskey in the girls' bathroom at school. OK, OK, maybe they'd had a problem. Eddie is dead and gone, said the rosebushes when Mary walked past them to get the mail. No he isn't, said the sewing machine. He might as well be, Mary thought. While she'd been in art school boiling the skins of dead rabbits to make glue, Eddie had been becoming famous. His nickname was the Booster. This was because he helped the Rockets achieve liftoff, Downie explained when Mary looked confused. All the women were madly in love with him. They had formed a fan club and for a while after he got hurt and was on the DL they tried to visit him before giving up in frustration. No one seemed to know where he was.

Tonight there would be tuna-noodle casserole for dinner; it was already sitting in the oven waiting for the oven to be turned on, the ingredients thoroughly mixed and topped with cornflakes. The bottle was in the drinks cabinet in the living room, on top of which Walter had put the globe of the known world. Sometimes in the evening he would stand above the globe and tap it lightly with his finger. He would set the globe spinning and then he would begin talking to himself. Though he talked softly, Mary could tell by the cadence of his speech that he was making plans.

All of a sudden for no apparent reason the sewing machine stopped. "Hey!" she said. When something like this occurred it could be a huge problem far away; it could be a small problem close to home. She awakened the console, checking for the emergency signal. To the sound of laughter, a man punched another man in the nose. Mary released the presser foot to remove the blouse but the blouse refused to budge. It wasn't until she looked under the slide plate and found an enormous snarl of pink thread all around the bobbin that she got up to pour herself a glass of whiskey. Her insides looked exactly like this, Mary knew. The doctor had told her a reproductive organ was busy growing outside itself, sending threads of itself wherever it wasn't supposed to. As long as it kept doing this she could never have another baby.

While Mary got drunk, the sorcerer was driving by the vacant lot at the foot of her old street. He could see Miss Vicks watching him from where she sat on one of the three benches the community association had placed there, one on each side of the lot to make it seem less vacant; as usual she was holding a leash that had a red dog attached to it. The lot formed an isosceles triangle with Miss Vicks's bench situated at the midpoint of a long side, facing the end of the street nearest her house and the house where Mary's parents used to live. For a while the house had been uninhabited and then a new family moved in with three small boys and a parakeet. Parakeets seemed to do well on the street. Aside from the house attached to number 37, houses there never stayed empty long—it was a desirable neighborhood.

The sorcerer couldn't help but notice that the dog let out a growl as his car sped past—in the rearview mirror he could see Miss Vicks petting its head to calm it. It wasn't the same dog she'd had when Mary was a girl, but the reaction was the same. "Slow down," Miss Vicks said. He could no longer see her but he could hear her perfectly, his ears being better than those of even moths or dolphins.

Now the streetlights came on. It wouldn't be dark for a while yet, though the sky already felt like it was filled with coming darkness. Miss Vicks had gotten up from the bench and was preparing to cross the overwide section of road between the lot and the holly bush at the foot of the street, waiting by the curb to let the sorcerer's car pass. She was pretending not to notice him, to keep her eyes cast down as if intent upon her dog, but he could feel the force of her interest. The sycamore trees were taller now, full of nests; the street was lined with parked cars and the sorcerer was driving too fast. He always drove too fast, not because he was in love with speed but because his mind was somewhere else.

Tonight the sorcerer's mind was on Marjorie Vicks—dear old Vicky—whose presence in his life had aroused a problem neither one of them could have anticipated or understood the full implications of. The problem already existed, its dark taproot extending deep into the future, its immense bloom already a thing of the past. Their affair had been a mistake, the sorcerer thought. A little breeze blew open the door of the Darling house, letting out lots of children. The sorcerer drove over a pothole; a shadow leaped from between two parked cars. It was twilight and there was the sound of a bump. The papers on the back seat came flying in a white fan around him.

He turned off the engine. How could this have happened? The community association had tried and failed to impose alternate-side-of-the-street parking. Some people had too many children and some people didn't have enough. There was no question the street had too many cars. The sorcerer stepped out of his car and looked to see if anyone was watching. There were procedures for fixing things like this but the last thing in the world he needed was an audience.

It was then that he saw that what he'd hit was no human child at all but something that looked like a toy, a bear in fact, yellow in color. It had leaped out in front of him—of that he was certain. The car had inflicted no damage the sorcerer could see. When he picked up the toy it was smiling at him, its little mouth slightly open and eager, revealing the tip of the tongue but no teeth. It held its forepaws against its chest in a posture the sorcerer knew signified submission. Mary had said she wanted a girl and the Yellow Bear seemed more like a boy, but then again it didn't have genitals. The sorcerer wiped it clean and put it on the passenger seat; a jingling sound came from it like it was a hard rubber cat toy with a bell inside. But the bear wasn't made of hard rubber. It was made of something soft and warm, more like skin.

Of course he recognized the creature for what it was right away; he'd been waiting for it. The Yellow Bear made its first appearance bobbing around on the swollen waters after the Great Flood, following which it disappeared for a while. It tended to show up in periods of unusual stress or upheaval. Even though it looked like it had been made in a factory by unskilled laborers, it had been forged in the Cradle of Civilization and was said to be the product of a collaboration between humans and machines, lending some credence to the belief that machines had been on the planet long before humans were capable of making them.

From the living room window of number 49 Miss Vicks stood watching, having been lured from her television program by the sound of squealing brakes. If she stood back she could remain invisible and still have a good view of the sorcerer. He continued to sit in the car, staring straight ahead toward the other end of the street where the trolleys ran.

Sometimes he looked down at whatever it was he'd leaned over to pick up and deposited on the seat beside him. The expression on his face was one she'd never seen there before and it surprised her, tender and clumsy, paternal almost.

It was dark enough now that the streetlights were turning the sycamores into stage trees with unnaturally bright green leaves, the moon and stars to props. You could see the blue lights of the scows, hear the high-pitched voices of boys playing baseball. After what seemed like a very long time the sorcerer started up the car and drove away.

Miss Vicks came onto her porch and sat in her glider. She'd shut the dachshund in the kitchen with a bone to keep him busy while she was spying on the sorcerer, and now the dog was whining to get out. All up and down the street girls were strolling, arms linked. The understanding was they were allowed to go anywhere as long as they behaved themselves—people had never gotten over the Rain of Beads, but these were obedient girls for the most part. The ones passing Miss Vicks's porch were singing a song from a hit musical: "The mist of May is in the gloaming, and all the clouds are holding still, so take my hand and let's go roaming through the heather on the hill." Most of them had sweet voices. Just one—and Miss Vicks thought she had a pretty good idea who it was—couldn't hold a tune but sang louder than the rest of them combined, spoiling everything.

"There may be other days as rich and rare, there may be other springs as full and fair . . ." The singing was loud enough that Miss Vicks smelled the photographer's horse before she heard it, the pleasant *tock-tock-tock* of its shod hooves on the macadam. Grass was at the heart of the smell, mediated by the smell of perspiration and saddle leather, combining to unlock a completely different set of memories from the ones unlocked by a lawn mower. Miss Vicks had been a passable equestrienne in her youth.

"Don't they know any better?" the photographer asked. He stopped on the grass verge in front of number 47. "Of all songs to be singing, why pick that?"

"It's a nice musical," Miss Vicks said, looking around. She had seen the show on Broadway, though whether it had been the original cast she couldn't remember. The only thing she could remember was that it had heralded a revival of the kilt as a popular item of apparel for women. The sorcerer's red taillights reached the far end of the street and he turned right without bothering to put on his turn signal. He was headed up the avenue, Miss Vicks knew, going home to Mary. He was tall, his arms long. He had thin tapered fingers like a surgeon, and he was going to slip them under Mary's skirt, gently, delicately.

"Nice?" said the photographer, hitching the horse to a telephone pole and beginning to erect his tripod. "What's nice about a place that disappears if you leave it? Who would want to live someplace where all it takes is one selfish person leaving home to make everyone vanish as if they never existed?" He seemed to be talking about the musical, but he was thinking about a story his mother used to tell him at bedtime. In the story the same thing happened. Afterward something that looked like smoke hung above the place, but it was really earth vapor, all that was left of the village once it sank into the ground.

"Have your picture taken on a real live cowpony!" the photographer called to the girls, but by now they were already past number 37 and out of earshot.

"Isn't it a little late for that?" said Miss Vicks.

"For some people, yes," he said.

"I mean isn't it too dark?"

"The night shots are the best," he explained, training the camera first on the horse, then on Miss Vicks. "They're the most atmospheric."

The horse craned its neck to stare at her. Its coat was dapple gray, its eyes blue. She could see the soft pink nostrils expand and contract, like something you'd want to stick your finger in. Maybe she was thinking this way because of the way she'd just been thinking about Mary and the sorcerer. The horse's skin really did look like velvet. "Go ahead. Climb on," the photographer said. "Give it a try."

Miss Vicks shook her head.

"I can tell you're dying to," he said.

"It's been years," she said, arising from the glider.

The horse slowly closed its eyes and opened them again, even slower, making it seem like the eyes that had been there before had been replaced with newer, better eyes. Miss Vicks put her foot in the stirrup and swung herself into the saddle.

"Look at me," the photographer said. "No need to smile." He focused the lens and as he began to shoot, Miss Vicks followed his instructions. She rarely smiled with her mouth, in any case. Then he walked over and gave the horse a pat on the rump. "Watch yourself," he said. "Between now and tomorrow lies a long, long night."

"Tomorrow?" said Miss Vicks. Already the horse was starting down the street toward the vacant lot, in the opposite direction of where the sorcerer had been headed. "I don't understand," she said.

"Tomorrow!" the photographer said. "You will understand tomorrow what that word means."

The girls stopped their singing long enough to stare. At some point they'd all been in Miss Vicks's classroom, but none of them had ever seen their teacher do anything like this before and they were embarrassed for her.

Disabled List

WHAT IS IT LIKE TO LIVE WITHOUT A SOUL? THE RO-bots gave this a lot of thought, it being their condition. Roy told Eddie that sometimes Cindy cried herself to sleep. How could she cry? How could she sleep, for that matter? Often what you don't have breaks your heart. The thing about souls is that with just the one exception, everyone has one. The gaping hole gets passed around, like the missing chair in musical chairs. Eddie had been a good person to begin with; the material part of his body including his brain cells and his memory couldn't forget that fact, even while the cold black wind of soullessness kept blowing through the empty space inside. Besides, baseball is a soulful game and at some point, despite how rich and famous he'd become, Eddie decided he'd had enough.

There had been a great tent of blue sky above the ballpark, there had been a field of green turf beneath his feet. Walter Woodard and Mary had just entered the owner's box. "I want it back," Eddie said, at the exact moment the batter connected with the ball, sending it high into the outfield. "Look!" Mary exclaimed, to which Walter replied, "We'll see about that."

BY NOW MARY HAD GROWN USED TO HEARING HER HUSBAND converse with people who weren't there. Still, she couldn't help but wonder who was to blame when Eddie collided with a teammate as they both came flying toward the same ball, crash-landing in front of the Alka-Seltzer sign.

It was midseason; the game had gone into extra innings. Midges clouded the stadium lights; the fans, in a body, held their breath. Of course Eddie had the ball, he always had the ball. The teammate should never have been there in the first place. A tie game and without Eddie's game-ending play the Rockets wouldn't have stood a chance; as it was, they ended up winning. The other player broke four ribs and had been back in the outfield for a while now—he wasn't anywhere near as popular as Eddie had been, but the accident happened long enough ago that Eddie's fans had all but forgotten him.

If the planets are in alignment sometimes what they do is crash into one another, Eddie's physical therapist explained. When that happens, she told him, you can't always see the damage.

She was standing at the foot of the bed, vigorously rubbing his feet with witch hazel, her yellow hair in a heavy braid that draped over one shoulder. When he'd asked her if that was why he was on the disabled list, she'd laughed. "Yes," she said, "I suppose you could say that." She seemed to find most of Eddie's questions hilarious.

For a while after the collision he had been nowhere, in the same place he'd been when he was a boy on the street and got taken away, a place that wasn't a place, without shape or color or dimension, but—for all that—so beautiful that for the rest of his life the memory of it could make him cry. It was like he saw nothing and then, very small and very far away at first, an avenue of trees and at its foot a triangle of grass with a small pool in the center, its water catching fire in the moonlight. There was a moon overhead, a gold-horned moon—there were fireflies, there were mosquitoes. A girl in a crown of stars was coming toward him, but before she could see who he was he slipped through his curtains of flesh.

Later he was tired; someone put him to bed. When he opened his eyes he saw a door and an arched window and a woman's head on the pillow beside him. Their brains weren't fully formed yet. He had been on his way somewhere; the gates to the city were barred but when he sounded his horn he'd been allowed to enter. To be brave and strong, he knew, was the most wonderful thing of all.

Something happened. The sky was deep black like at midnight but with a sun in it. The bladed leaves of the plants, the twigs of the sycamores, the tree trunks, and the whole world radiated from where he lay curled on his side looking out the arched window, everything just beginning to settle back into stillness after a period of terrible agitation, as if for a while nothing had remained itself but had spun into shining bits and the bits themselves had gotten mixed together, so that whoever he was lying there had pieces mixed into him of trees and plants and sky.

He was pretty sure he'd never before seen the woman who was lying beside him, but when she moved closer there was something about the temperature of her skin that felt familiar.

"I didn't think you were awake," he said.

"I'm not," she replied, and they both laughed.

Laughing, he could feel the gate of his jaw move, reminding him that he was living in a body. An image arose in his brain that made no sense, a field lit from above and the sky farther away than usual, pasted across the top of impossibly high palings. People were screaming with excitement and there was a falling star coming at him, falling right toward him through the black night sky. He was supposed to catch it. It was his job to catch it and he didn't.

Instead it got trapped behind one of the room's many

woven tapestries and the sound it made trying to escape kept him from falling back asleep. The room was round in shape, the walls built of stone. The tapestries quivered; he was aware of his tongue in his mouth, how heavy it was, and there was a taste like honey at the back of it.

"Eddie!" a woman's voice said. "Enough is enough. You have to wake up now!"

The physical therapist wore a uniform like a nurse would wear, though she also had on black fishnet stockings and high-heeled shoes; temptingly, as if it were whiskey, she unscrewed the cap from a bottle of smelling salts and waved it in his face.

Immediately he felt overexcited and enormously uncertain, exactly the way he had the time everyone went to play hide-and-seek in the Woodard Estate and no one came to find him. He was still in his hiding place under a lilac bush when a group of girls walked past on their way home. "There's someone in there," Mary said, but when she pulled back the creeper and saw it was Eddie sitting there crying, she told the other girls she'd been imagining things.

Before he got taken away, he'd been a nervous boy. He had trouble sleeping unless his mother read to him. There was the pestering sound of branches on his bedroom window, there were eyes suspended in the rose trellis. At first getting up to pee was more than he could handle, but the physical therapist had a urinal. When he was a boy sometimes he wet the bed.

Now it was the therapist who was reading to him. "Your biography," she said, jokingly. She flashed him a quick look at the book, which did in fact have his name on the cover. A fairy told a boy that the piece of fabric she cut from the hem of her skirt and gave him as a special present could be stretched to any size imaginable, but that he should never stretch it unless he knew what he wanted to make with it, because if he just started doing it for the fun of it, it would go on stretching and stretching forever. Of course like all fairies she was counting on the fact that the boy would disobey her.

"What kind of a special present is that?" Eddie asked.

"This is not just any world," his therapist told him. "Haven't you been listening? It's thy world. It's my world. Don't you remember?" She opened the book to show him a picture of someone dressed in a pale green cloak with a crown of lightning bugs in her hair, sitting in a blue boat being rowed into a dark grotto by a boy wearing a red cap. "I've been with you ever since that day, Eddie," the therapist said, and she tapped him on the chest in the place where the pocket would be if he were wearing a shirt.

"That's very kind of you," Eddie said.

"It's my job," the therapist told him. "Kindness has nothing to do with it."

He had been a boy when he was here before, that much was clear. When he came back his mother and father were sitting at the card table in the living room, playing canasta the way they did every night.

"Are you thirsty?" his mother had asked. "There's some lemonade in the fridge."

"I'm going to meld," his father had said, like someone preparing to do something shameful.

Eddie fell asleep and when he woke he was lying in the same bed. The bed was unusually large, or maybe it seemed that way because there was no one else in it with him. For some reason he could see the wall hangings better than he had earlier. They stretched from near the roof all the way to the floor and showed scenes of events from the Great Division— the Descent of the Aquanauts, the Rain of Beads, Space Drift, the Seven Dormant Birds of Winter. The arched window, covered by a curtain, was no longer visible. To Eddie it

felt like being inside a tent; he had no idea whether it was day
or night, though he thought he could hear chirping sounds,
wheels creaking, a voice raised giving directions.

After a while his therapist reappeared to take his temperature. While he was lying there with the thermometer in
his mouth she ran her hand through his hair, smoothing it
off his forehead but without looking at what she was doing,
moving her lips and staring into space like a typist. When
he asked her how he was doing she told him he was doing
fine. When he asked her when he could go back to playing
baseball she laughed.

"Am I going to have to tickle you to get you to laugh,
too?" she asked.

"I didn't think I was being funny," Eddie said.

"Well, you were," she said. "You rascal."

Sometimes she pulled aside the tapestry that showed the
Rain of Beads to reveal the console in the wall behind it.
The images on all the tapestries were disturbing, but Eddie
thought the Rain of Beads was the worst. It was as if you
were lying on your back on the ground looking up at the
sky at the exact moment the rain began to fall, the weaver
having created the illusion of a three-dimensional pyramid
of many-colored drops, the bigger drops forming the base
of the pyramid, which was coming right at you, and behind
them increasingly smaller drops, rising to the very tip of the
pyramid, which was also the silver base of the scow.

The therapist would activate the console so Eddie could
watch the Rockets. He would lie there and look at the
picture—mostly he loved it when the camera showed the
ballpark from above, touchingly small and brightly lit, car-
peted in bright green grass his teammates jumped around on
like fleas. When the camera shifted to show them closer up,
swinging at the ball or diving to catch a line drive into center, he was less interested. It was unclear whether his thera-

pist wanted to lift or lower his spirits when she did this—her motives remained a mystery to Eddie, as did her program of physical therapy, which consisted of rubbing first his feet and then his calves and then his thighs and when he was fully aroused, taking him into her mouth.

It seemed like it was always sunny in the ballpark, the stands completely filled with happy cheering fans. The Rockets had adopted a new way of wearing their hair, with razor-straight side parts and triangle-shaped sideburns. Occasionally the picture on the console would switch to show the box where the team owner sat with his wife and their little girl, who had ended up being quite cute despite the way she started out. The owner's wife looked exactly like Mary, only older.

She *was* Mary—Eddie knew this because the therapist had made fun of him the first time he mentioned the resemblance. Mary wore a paisley scarf and sunglasses; sometimes she was eating a hot dog, sometimes she was drinking a beer. The little girl seemed unable to sit still. Once Eddie saw the team owner yank the little girl's arm hard, making her cry out. Then the picture switched back to the field, where one of Eddie's old teammates was stealing second, and by the time it returned to the box, Mary and the little girl were gone.

But that had been another lifetime, the therapist reminded Eddie whenever he grew melancholy. Another lifetime and not even the same ecosystem.

He had no idea how long he'd been on the disabled list—the DL, as they referred to it. Usually if someone was on the DL long enough it was as if he'd died. At some point Eddie noticed the Rockets stopped having his number printed in commemoration on their sleeves. He had been number 24, in honor of the house where he grew up.

One day he woke to find a large white dog on the bed

beside him. It lay facing the foot of the bed, its forepaws extended in front of it sphinx fashion, its mouth open, panting. When Eddie made a move to sit up the dog let out a low musical growl, not exactly threatening but not encouraging either. He could feel the warmth of its body against his own through the sheets; when he moved to get closer it craned its head around and looked him in the eye, meaningfully, the way an animal does when it wants a person to do something.

Eventually the dog jumped from the bed, nudged the door open with its nose, and disappeared. Eddie could hear its toenails clicking down a flight of steps. It wasn't a real dog—he knew that. It was very old, maybe even a thousand, older than a breastplate of hammered bronze or a virus. With the door open Eddie could see the inside of the stairwell, which was made of stone like his room and had a tall thin window in it showing a slit of cloudy sky. Cautiously he lowered himself to the floor—the bed was quite high, the floor also made of stone.

The stairwell was chilly, the window without a pane. Eddie walked over to it and looked out. He hadn't left the room since he first arrived; everything he needed, including food and a slop bucket, was brought in while he slept and removed while he slept. "You are barking up the wrong tree," his therapist informed him tersely the first time he tried thanking her. "I am your physical therapist." She seemed to be implying that any other activity was far beneath her.

I must be inside the water tower, he thought. Growing up, he had only seen it from the outside, its front door sealed with concrete and weeds sticking through the windows. Eddie and the other boys liked to climb to the crenellated top of the tower where they got a good view of the neighborhood, including into the community center where they could watch the girls getting undressed for their ballet lesson. Mary usually tried to hide herself behind a locker, but she wasn't always successful. The boys stopped climbing after one of them fell and cracked his skull in two.

Now the stairwell window gave an unbroken view of a wide plain dotted with barbed gray-green shrubs, the earth's curve at the horizon so faint it was almost invisible but undeniably *there*, a queenly entourage of clouds in procession above it. Otherwise all he could see were the barbed gray-green shrubs and, if he leaned out the window, a large haystack. The community center must be behind me, Eddie thought, but there wasn't a window on that side of the room.

He started down the stairs, moving slowly and cautiously, trying not to make any noise. It wasn't as if he'd been held prisoner exactly, but he had a clear sense that he would get in trouble if his therapist were to see what he was doing. The stairs went on forever, around and around the inside of the tower. The only actual room in the building, he realized, was the one where he'd been kept, near the roof.

Eventually he heard two women having what sounded like a heated discussion just beyond the tower door.

"She's proud," one woman said, "in case no one noticed."

"She cured my shingles," said the other woman.

"Shingles cure themselves," said the first.

The lower Eddie climbed, the better his legs worked. He started to move faster, hoping to catch up with the women and perhaps ask them a few questions, but by the time he got to the bottom of the stairwell they were nowhere to be seen.

It was a fine afternoon and some village maidens were tending their sheep on a grassy knoll at the edge of town. Eddie passed the haystack he'd seen from above and realized it was burning. He passed a rearing horse, saddled but riderless, a group of schoolgirls clustered together, dressed in bright blue uniforms. "Watch out," one of them said, "don't let it touch you," *it* meaning Eddie, though on reflection it almost seemed as if they didn't even know he was there.

Motherhood

MARY LOVED HER DAUGHTER FROM THE MINUTE SHE laid eyes on her; she held her to her cheek and smiled. "The baby's tired. She wants to go to sleep now," Mary told Walter. She put the Yellow Bear in an old pink doll dress and carried it upstairs with her, then she got into bed with it and turned off the light.

In the morning when he brought Mary her breakfast tray of tea and toast he found her propped on her pillow, the bear at her breast. She was no longer smiling but had tears running down her cheeks. "I don't know if I can do it," Mary told him. The jingling sound the sorcerer had first heard when he set the bear down on the passenger seat was very loud now, ear-splitting. "She won't stop," Mary said. "She needs something from you, too. That's how babies get made, in case you forgot."

"She's no baby, she's a toy," Walter said, but when he went to show Mary the rubber seam running across the top of the bear's head, the baby sank its teeth into his thumb clear to the bone.

Later, when Mary had cried herself to sleep, the sorcerer snuck the bear from her breast and filled it with the substance he'd been keeping secret all this time in the jar in his basement workshop. "Pabulum," he told Mary when she ·

asked, because now there could be no question, the little girl was alive and thriving and cute as a button.

"What shall we call her?" Mary asked.

Because they couldn't agree on a name, they decided to call her Blue-Eyes.

People often said that motherhood was the hardest job a person would ever have. Mary was in total agreement, an attitude she was sharing with Cindy XA as they walked side by side up the Avenue, pushing their baby carriages, the old-fashioned hooded kind that had made a comeback recently. The new crop of babies found it impossible to prosper if there was too much light or too many people staring them in the face. They had to be allowed to live their lives independent of their mothers in the shadow country underneath their carriage hoods that smelled, sweetly, of fabric softener sheets. "I don't know about you," Mary said to Cindy, "but I haven't gotten a full night's sleep ever since Blue-Eyes . . ."

She didn't know how to finish the sentence—it wasn't like her daughter had actually been *born*. The leaves of the ginkgo trees on either side of the entrance door to Mr. Costello's haberdashery were like little yellow hands grabbing at her as she walked by—Mary knew they were exactly the kind of thing that would drive Blue-Eyes crazy. The seasons kept turning. There was nothing you could do about it.

"I'm getting one of those for Roy," Cindy told Mary, pointing at a madras-plaid cummerbund cinched around the waist of a beige mannequin with smooth beige hair and beige eyes and a beige mouth. "We're lucky our husbands have kept their boyish physique."

Mary couldn't picture Walter wearing a plaid cummerbund unless maybe he was naked and fooling around.

From the back of the store, Mr. Costello gestured toward the mannequin and waved Cindy in, but she shook her head, pointing at the baby carriage. "We've got to keep moving," she mouthed. The need to keep moving was paramount with this newest crop of babies. Once the carriage had started moving, the baby would fly into a rage—and rage is not too strong a word for what overtook these babies—should the carriage come to a halt. Its head would expand like a balloon blown overfull of air. Sometimes its eyes would roll around and around in the sockets until all you could see were the backs of the eyeballs, white and crisscrossed with veins.

Mary loved Blue-Eyes so much that just thinking of her daughter made her feel like her insides were being vacuumed out. It was love and it was terror rolled up in one, the love feeding the terror, and the terror feeding itself with thoughts of all the terrible things that could happen to a helpless little girl, that had happened to little girls in the past and that were continuing to happen to little girls all the time. "Do you have trouble sleeping, too?" Mary asked Cindy.

"It's different for me," Cindy reminded Mary.

When a robot is hurt by human insensitivity—when the human fails to remember that robots never sleep, for example—then the robot might not bother to modulate its voice or make it sound like the product of a human voice box. Cindy's voice still sounded human but it also sounded as if it had gotten trapped in a box made of metal on a planet in another galaxy and was beating against the sides of the box trying to get out.

"I'm sorry," Mary said, and she was. Whatever the truth was about Cindy's mechanism, Mary knew the robot was sensitive and could experience something exactly like pain. Her skin would shimmer and grow dull.

"It's just that I'm having such a hard time lately," Mary said. "I always used to think the end of the world was at hand. We all did, right? But then it didn't end. It just kept on going, even after each of those endings foretold by some prophet. Now I'm constantly expecting it—every single moment I'm braced, like right now, thinking, this is going to be the last moment everything will still be the way it is with the sun above the trolley barn and Mr. Costello's ginkgo trees and the cobblestones on the Avenue. I love Blue-Eyes so much it's like I can't help imagining the worst. Sometimes I even think it would be better if she didn't exist."

There was one particular book Mary read to her daughter at bedtime. Every time they came to the picture of a pair of elephants dressed up like human beings on their way out of a house, Blue-Eyes would wave at Mary—sweetly, plaintively—and mouth the word *bye*. Mary didn't think her own mother had ever read her to sleep. Her mother had been a night owl, meaning she stayed awake until all hours drinking highballs and watching television talk shows, hearing "personalities" promote their views on a variety of topics they knew nothing about but that Mary's mother then ardently espoused. She wasn't stupid, she was an alcoholic—it had taken Mary a while to realize this.

By now the two women had reached the top of the Avenue. At this point they could fork left around the trolley barn in the direction of Mary's house, or fork right down Rex to the Woodard Estate. From somewhere up above came the scissoring sound of raptors doing maneuvers.

"Do you want to come back with me for lunch?" Mary asked.

"Listen to me, Mary," Cindy said, and now her voice was inside Mary's brain. It was like that time at recess on the swing set when Cindy linked arms with her and began swinging and the next thing Mary knew she was in the dark corner of the playground the trash blew into. That had been so long ago—she'd had no idea then where her life was headed.

"Do you know what would happen if even one single molecule of Blue-Eyes didn't exist?" Cindy's voice asked Mary from inside Mary's brain.

They had turned right toward the Woodard Estate, without further discussion. "Nothing?" Mary said. Blue-Eyes had already lost several of her sharp pointed baby teeth and Mary had seen no reason to keep them. Her hair, too— Blue-Eyes had lost most of the first, colorless hair that had grown into her smooth bald scalp. Her hair was brown now, like Mary's.

"No," Cindy said. "I don't mean a molecule that gets thrown away or turned into something else. I mean a molecule that existed and suddenly doesn't exist. One single molecule, that's all it will take. One little hole. *That's* how the world will end, Mary. When you think you're imagining the worst you aren't even close. Do you hear me? This world. Why don't you ask your husband if you don't believe me."

"My husband?"

"Stop answering questions with questions!"

They had entered the estate on a narrow trail that cut through what had once been a magnificent cedar hedge trimmed to resemble a high stone wall with topiary urns at regular intervals. Now the hedge had no obvious shape at all, some sections being very tall or very short or sending forth irregular branches in all directions like the mind of a madman. This was what Walter's father had turned out to be, matter—as is so often the case—having no alternative but to imitate mind. Whatever Walter was, he wasn't a madman, of that Mary felt certain.

The path through the hedge went on and on, more like a tunnel, and was laced with roots; small creatures raced past, brushing against Mary's ankles in their hurry to get wherever they were going, which seemed to be away from the estate and not into it. As far ahead as she could see the path was dappled with pale white spots that shifted when she wasn't looking at them. It was like sunlight was falling onto the path through the interwoven cedar boughs above

her head, but Mary knew this couldn't be possible since at
some point not long after they'd entered the path, night had
fallen. Blue-Eyes was wide awake and had raised herself into
a seated posture unassisted, something the books claimed
she wouldn't be doing for another six months. Cindy was
nowhere to be seen.

"This is ridiculous," Mary said. It was becoming more
and more difficult to push the carriage across the tangled
roots, not to mention the horrible sound—as if its soul was
being squeezed into the dirt—that came out of one of the
escaping creatures when she accidentally ran it over with
the carriage. She ought to be in her kitchen making dinner. Walter would be arriving home any minute; tonight
was fish sticks. Of course she hadn't brought a flashlight—
she hadn't thought she'd need one. She had forgotten how
quickly the days grew short this time of year. If there was a
moon Mary couldn't see it.

She came to a halt and Blue-Eyes began to scream. "Stop
it!" Mary said. "Stop it!" She was trying to turn the carriage
around but one of its wheels had gotten caught on something. "Just be patient," she said, and Blue-Eyes screamed
louder. "I'm trying," Mary said.

"You have to try harder, Mother," said Blue-Eyes. "Weren't
you listening to"—and here she said a name Mary knew was
supposed to be "Cindy." Blue-Eyes was sitting all the way up
now and was much too big to be riding in a baby carriage.

They were no longer in the tunnel but in a clearing, an immense meadow that appeared to have been recently mowed
and was dotted with several large haystacks, the whole thing
surrounded by cedar trees. It was as if the narrow space
they'd been in had suddenly swelled and the cedars along
with it, the wall of trees getting thinner and thinner and
moving farther and farther away, like a balloon being blown
up—when she thought about it, Mary realized she couldn't

remember ever coming out of the tunnel. The sky, on the other hand, didn't look anything like the sky had looked before. It was as immense as the meadow, with a strangely bulging sliver of moon and loads of falling stars. The wind began to blow.

"Pssst," something said very close at hand.

"Cindy?" Mary looked around but there was no one there.

"Pssst," she heard again.

There at her feet lay the body of a big gray hare. By now everyone had come to take the hares for granted, the fact that wherever you went there they were, sitting up tall and staring into space with their huge gray eyes. They seemed to have appeared for some purpose—no one could tell you what—though the blond boy from the academy had capitalized on the mystery. In his one-man show his new paintings showed the hares larger than life-size, towering over everything, beginning with not-so-very-big things like birdbaths or mailboxes and ending up with houses and office buildings.

The hare at Mary's feet seemed bigger than whatever it was she thought she had run over with the carriage. Its dead body frightened her, the glazed surface of its upward-facing eye reminding her of Eddie's eyes that night after the prom. She tried to remember how long it had been since she'd last seen him, but she couldn't. She thought it had been at the ballpark, before he got injured. She used to like watching him stand at the plate, wondering whether he knew she was there in the stands watching him. When they were younger she could tell from the way he stood, the curve at the small of his back—his body was attentive to her even if his mind was on the game. Then again, maybe the last time she saw him had been on the street before she moved away. Eddie had been wearing his Rockets uniform—she remembered the same photographer who had taken their picture at the prom posing him with the lawn mower at the foot of number 24's extremely steep lawn. That was probably it, Mary thought. She still had the picture that she'd cut out of the newspaper; it was captioned "Local Hero." After the photographer packed up his camera, Eddie went back inside, leaving his father to do the job.

The mower's sound was one you almost never heard anymore, Mary thought, unless you counted the mowerlike sound of the raptors. The brightness of the sky, the freshness of the breeze, the forsythia in full bloom, like offshoots of sunlight. The winding of the horn, the horn in the wood. *Dieu que le son du cor est triste au fond du bois!*

"I'm hungry, Mother," Blue-Eyes said. She handed Mary a knife with a curved blade. "I never get enough to eat."

"Where did you get this?" Mary asked, before she remembered that Blue-Eyes couldn't talk yet. Something else was talking—that had to be the explanation.

"Your milk is like water. Nursing at your breast is like trying to get water from a hose with knots in it."

Mary took the knife her daughter had handed her and cut the hare's body into pieces.

The Four Horsewomen

YOU KNOW WHAT HAPPENED NEXT, RIGHT? JANICE
asked. She stood there balanced on one leg in what had
come to be called the Mary Pose, after the famous Mary who
had lived in number 47.

But no one knew; girls never know what happens next.
Days went by, weeks, years even. Everything in life stood
poised like Mary on the verge of what was possible. For example Janice had a boyfriend—no one could have predicted
this. He went to Our Mother of Consolation and used to be
one of the boys on bikes who appeared on the street to throw
eggs at anyone who didn't get out of the way. A little girl
jumping rope opened her mouth to scream and an egg went
in and after a while a chick hatched in her stomach.

No one was interested in trading cards anymore. All the
good trades had been made, the black horse and the white
horse at last together in a pack in the bottom of the cigar
box in the back of Janice's closet. At some point her mother
decided to have a new closet system put in. She didn't admit
it to herself, but her mother was preparing for the day when
Janice would get married and leave home for good and she
could take over the closet as her own. The cigar box was hidden under a pair of toe shoes and a tutu and a black velvet riding helmet and a ton of foil candy wrappers from back when

Janice used to lie stomach-down in the closet, producing one foil-wrapped chocolate egg after another from somewhere underneath her like an exotic type of frog. Janice's mother put everything except the candy wrappers in a carton along with her fox stole and several *Reader's Digest* condensed books and took the carton to church for the Christmas bazaar.

The obsession with trading cards had been replaced with a fad for writing novels about horses. The novels were composed in the same marbleized notebooks that had once been fashionable for schoolwork. The system was: one novel per notebook. Fathers still were forced to buy cigars they would never smoke, but now it was so their daughters could enter a contest sponsored by the cigar company and win a racehorse. "Lightning Bolt," "Black Dancer," "Speed Demon," "Nightmare"—any one of these names could be a winner, plus they also made excellent titles for the novels. "White Cloud."

"In a dank cave in the mountains of the west a baby foal named White Cloud was born. It arose slowly on its dainty legs, its fetlocks wobbling with the superhuman effort, its mother, the dapple-gray mare who had just found sanctuary there from the wrath of the thunderstorm, was nickering softly to it."

Horses aren't born in caves, someone pointed out. Also, a foal *is* a baby.

It was like a club: Saturday afternoon they all met with their notebooks in the park at the foot of the street and took turns reading their novels aloud. The park had once been a vacant lot where people's dogs defecated without anyone bothering to pick up after them, but over time the community association had brought about a great many improvements, including planting a flower garden more or less at the center of the triangle and moving the three benches so they faced in at the flowers rather than out at the traffic. An old-fashioned street lamp was added later and a koi pool with a plaque on it commemorating the famous baseball player who had lived on the street and had once been Mary's true love.

Superhuman doesn't apply to horses, Janice said.

Something in her tone made the author of "White Cloud" bristle. This was a curly-haired girl everyone knew wanted to be a writer when she grew up. I know that, the girl said.

That also happens to be a run-on sentence, Janice added.

She wasn't a member of the club but often wandered through on her way to or from meeting her boyfriend. This was where she said she was headed or had been—no one knew for sure, only that she dressed the part of girlfriend with her camel-hair coat and tartan tam and brown leather pocketbook with its clasp shaped like a horseshoe. As Janice had gotten older she hadn't gotten prettier. Her face was round like risen dough someone had stuck fingers in to make eyes. Still, she wore coins in her loafers, which meant she was going steady.

If she wore them in her eyes it would mean she was dead, the curly-haired girl whispered, not loud enough for Janice to hear.

There were no longer any flowers blooming in the garden, and sometimes overnight a sheet of ice formed above the two gigantic vermilion fish in the koi pool. The fish seemed to hang suspended without moving a muscle—some of the little girls, the ones who weren't really club members but whose older sisters were—found the fish frightening. The only way you could tell they were alive was how every now and then one or the other of them would release a long dark string of excrement into the pool. The string would drift for a while and then break apart, making a horrible brown cloud.

I used to take riding lessons, Janice said. I know a lot about horses. I had a natural seat, Miss Haines told me.

She would rise and fall at the triple bar, the water-jump,

the gate, the imitation wall, her hands buried in the flying mane firm on the stout muscles of her horse's neck. He was a natural jumper, Janice said. She did not need to dictate to him. They cleared the wall together, wildly, ludicrously high, with savage effort and glory, and twice the power and the force that was needed.

Those aren't her words, whispered the curly-haired girl. That's *National Velvet*.

Almost everyone knew that at Miss Haines's riding stable Janice had been put on the oldest and slowest horse, a tall white gelding with a tail so thin you could see the bone through the hair. As Janice posted around and around the ring, holding the reins stiffly to either side like a dowser, Miss Haines stood at the rail, shouting directions. Janice was a terrible rider; she was afraid of horses, of all animals really.

You think you're so smart, Janice said. She pointed at the sky and a few girls looked in the direction of her finger.

What was that? someone asked, but there wasn't anything there aside from an airship and a long thin airship-shaped cloud.

If you have to ask, I'm not telling, Janice said. If you have to ask, it's too late.

Too late for what? someone asked.

For a very important date, said someone else.

Go ahead, Janice said. Laugh why don't you. She told everyone to thank their lucky stars she was there to laugh at. We were all too young to remember, but for a while after the Rain of Beads there weren't any girls anywhere. On the street you could hear the sounds of boys playing baseball and sprinklers watering lawns and crickets rubbing their hind legs together and ice cubes clinking in highballs. So many of the sounds everyone expected to hear were there that it took a while before anyone realized the high-pitched sound of girls' voices was missing. The boys' voices hadn't changed yet—that might have been part of the problem. But it was also true that no one wanted to admit what had happened.

The saddest thing, Janice said, was that everyone was very sad but no one could talk to anyone else about it. They were so sad they didn't notice how some of the new girls were coming through wormholes instead of birth canals. It was hard to tell since often the wormholes were inside the mothers. Even the doctors couldn't tell the difference.

That was the first generation of girls, Janice said, and I was in it.

Most of them were regular, but some of them were not one hundred percent girls; the only way to know for sure was when they played horse. You've all played horse, right?

We club members found it embarrassing to admit to ever having played such a babyish game, even though we had loved it when we did. Playing horse was like being caught in the act of "talking" for a doll or a pet—the only way it worked was if everyone was playing and there was no audience. To play horse you held your arms out with your elbows bent and your wrists cocked for the reins. On a real horse the reins would stay at the horse's withers, but since the rest of the horse was you, this was the only way to clarify the separation between horse and rider, a distinction that was, in any case, fluid and boundaryless and subject to infinite change. The best part of the game was executing different gaits; it was also tricky to accomplish this on two legs instead of four. Cantering was the best.

You know what a centaur is, don't you? Janice asked. She handed round sticks of gum but not everyone took one—most young people's gums bled easily from what was said to be vitamin C deficiency.

A ballplayer? asked one of the little sisters.

Not *that* kind of centaur, said someone else.

You mean a mythological creature, said the curly-haired girl, but since the *National Velvet* remark Janice had ceased to acknowledge her presence.

When the first generation of girls played horse they made the vacant lot into a racecourse. Back then the lot was a mess. No one mowed the grass and it was full of dog shit. Drunks often passed out on the benches, leaving behind paper bags with empty gin bottles inside. The girls had to watch where they put their hooves without losing sight of the other horses. They'd also been trained by their parents to keep an eye on the sky—everyone was still vigilant after the Rain of Beads. It was the job of a diabetic girl who'd lost one of her legs and hadn't gotten her new one yet to shoot the pistol to start the race. She used a real starter pistol one of the other girls had found in her father's workbench.

The gun went off and the girls began to gallop. They were just girls, most of them, in their shorts and T-shirts and silver shoon, their manes and tails French-braided and their tack polished to a high gloss with saddle soap.

From his vantage point atop the water tower the sorcerer was watching the race through his telescope, which he'd set up in the gap between two of the crenellation's stone teeth. The sorcerer had never been interested in little girls; he was watching their necks, not their bottoms. It isn't in an animal's nature to look up, Janice said—I bet you didn't know that. Animals don't have the muscles and bones needed to move that way. By noticing which of the girls tilted their necks and which ones didn't, the sorcerer could tell which girls running around the lot were girls and which were centaurs.

The Centaurs are ahead of the Rockets, said the same little sister, breathless with excitement at having something to add to the conversation.

Shhh, said her older sister but Janice wasn't paying attention.

Everyone kept looking up because they thought danger came from the sky, she said, since that was where it came from the last time. This is because the Greeks had it backward, and no matter how hard humans try thinking otherwise, they still think like Greeks. For the Greeks, when you looked ahead all you saw was the past. It was like the past *was* the future. It never occurred to anyone that they ought to be looking at their own daughters.

Four of the girls weren't real girls at all.

Would we recognize their names? someone asked. Did they live on the street?

I told you before, Janice said. No names. Why do you always want to hear names? Does that bush have a name? Does that tree? How about those fish?

It's just that she hasn't *thought* of any names, said the girl who wanted to be a writer.

The fish are called Mr. Poopie and Mrs. Poopie said the littlest sister.

Janice surveyed the group with enormous pity. If I told you the names it would make your brains explode, she said. She took a seat in the middle of a bench, using her wide hips to bump aside the girls who were sitting there. Then she opened her pocketbook and removed a small Bible that had to be unzipped to be read. Janice's boyfriend was very religious; she went to Bible study class with him. He used to be planning to be a priest before he met Janice.

Some people think what you're supposed to do in life is fill yourself up with loads of things like names, the more the better. But that's not how it works. In here, she said, unzipping the book, it says there will be ten thousand times ten thousand angels and so on milling around the throne. In Bible days they thought ten thousand was an impossibly huge number. Like in the song, when we've been here ten thousand years bright shining as the sun. When you think about it though, ten thousand isn't all that much. When you compare it with eternity, ten thousand's nothing. And nothing's exactly what you're supposed to be filling yourself up with.

The girls' horse parts were invisible to everyone except themselves. One was white and one was red and one was black and one didn't have any color at all. I guess you could say the red one was roan. Because they looked like girls no one thought they weren't. Eventually it was time for dinner and everyone went home—the centaurs lived in numbers 22 and 23 and 35 and 44. Many families were having spaghetti and meatballs as a special treat, it being Saturday. Aside from the family of atheists in number 22, they all said grace first. Bless oh Lord this food to our use and us to thy service.

And make us ever mindful of the needs of others, someone finished, but Janice was too involved now to hear anything but herself.

What each family saw was nothing like what the four centaurs saw. Three of these families saw a girl sitting with her head bowed over her plate of spaghetti, saying grace. These girls were especially attractive physical specimens. The one with white horse parts looked Scandinavian like her parents, the one with roan parts, Irish. The black centaur's father's father had been an African king. The atheists' daughter was albino but even so her parents watched adoringly as she arranged her paper napkin on her lap and began twirling strands of spaghetti around her fork. Her mother called her my little fragrant one, due to the sweet aroma of her skin. The dining rooms were all identical, the houses having been built at the same time by the same developer. An identical light fixture hung above each dining room table, a kind of chandelier with six "arms" and six round bulbs that were aimed at the ceiling instead of the table, creating an interesting pattern overhead but making it hard to see what you were eating.

Ours has a dimmer switch, someone said.

The dimmer switches got added later, said someone else.

Do you want to talk about dimmer switches or do you want to hear what happened? Janice asked.

For the centaurs it wasn't like being inside a dining room. For them it was like being in an open place without anything in it where the sky was thin and transparent like a colored mist with blue and green and yellow stripes you could see the moon and stars through. Then the sky was gone and they could see all the way to the beginning of time and the end of time. These are the same thing, as everyone knows who came into this universe via a wormhole.

In the Rain of Beads girls got taken away. Blue Boy and Pinkie were gone forever—or if not forever it might as well have been. That was years and years ago, Janice said, adopting a matronly tone.

This time nothing was taken away. This time something was added.

The girls were all fine.

It was a fine evening and they were exercising their legs in the space that had opened for them between the beginning and end of time. To their families it looked like they were sitting at the dinner table, using their forks to twirl spaghetti or chase a meatball around and around the plate. What a wonderful thing it is to have a daughter, the fathers were thinking; the mothers were amazed but critical. The white girl could never keep herself clean, the roan had to watch her weight. The king's granddaughter's teeth needed straightening. The albino girl was allergic to everything. This was only true at the dinner table—otherwise they were without flaw. The plain they raced across extended uphill to a walled city with a tower and downhill to the seashore, where each summer for a month or so their families rented cottages with a view of the water.

You never know what you're going to find in a rental cottage, Janice said. Once she found a rosary sewed to the bottom of her mattress. Once she found a miniature golf pencil, a pair of stained underpants, and a piece of paper with "clams" written on it in her bureau drawer. Once someone used a *Reader's Digest* condensed book about a girl named Stephanie who was the same age as her brother and who died of leukemia to prop open the bathroom window. Last summer there was a conch shell on the kitchen counter with its animal still inside, the exact size and weight of a human thumb.

The man in number 37 wrote a book about shells, someone said.

He was famous, said the curly-haired girl. He won some prizes and then he moved away.

No one ever thinks their stay anywhere is going to be cut short, Janice replied, and everyone knew she was thinking about her brother.

Shadows moved around all over the plain but if you tried to see what was casting them there was nothing there. The four horsewomen cast no shadows—they never do. This is how they differ from the four horsemen. They cast no shadow, they leave no hoofprints. The evil they bring is harder to pin down, often seeming more good than evil. One of them loves to fatten you up with butter and cream so you'll turn out fatter than she is. Flattery is involved. Filth weighs down the crimson drugget, the blind slats—no one gets things cleaner! No one is more beautiful either—if only you weren't depressed. The pale one is the best nurse ever. You'd better not get better or she won't have anything to do.

They can show up anytime, Janice said, in any group. The only way to stop them is if the horse parts get the strangles.

Like a lighthouse she rotated her head in one smooth mechanical operation, the beam of her gaze landing on each of us in turn. Then to everyone's amazement she reached into her pocketbook and came up with a pack of cigarettes, took one out, lit it, and began to smoke.

What about the sorcerer? someone asked.

What about him? Janice sounded irritable. She blew smoke rings and consulted her wristwatch, busy giving the impression of being a busy person—a busy *woman*—with things to do, places to go, a whole life to live that had nothing to do with any of us.

Once those four get loose even a sorcerer can't do a thing to change the course of events. Like the woman in number 50 who jumped in front of a train last Easter—everyone knew the story. She had been a young mother of two; her husband worked in the city and she stayed home with the children. All the parents agreed she was a devoted mother and an excellent homemaker. Their house was the last one on the street and it had a large side yard that she kept neat as a pin. Not long after the family moved into the neighborhood the husband planted a tree in the middle of the yard and staked it with wires. No one was to blame—these things happen, like the cocker spaniel in number 21 who ran out in front of the bread truck or the man in number 30 who woke up one day and couldn't move his legs. Like all the kids absent at school—more every day. If the little boy had told his mother when he cut his stomach on the wire maybe things would have gone differently. But he kept it a secret. And then he got lockjaw and died.

No he didn't, someone said.

I heard she was fooling around with the man in number 52, said someone else.

Fooling around, said a little sister, and all the little sisters began to giggle.

If you're so smart why don't you tell the story? Janice asked. She ground out the cigarette under the heel of her loafer. It was starting to get dark; it got dark earlier and earlier with the approach of the holidays. As if to reinforce this fact the street lamp came on at the exact moment that a white car with a salmon-pink roof pulled up alongside the curb. I've got to go now, Janice said, reaching into her pocketbook for a tube of lipstick. The boyfriend kept the engine idling while he rolled down the window—the light from the street lamp reflected off his eyeglasses and made him look like a lemur. He was wearing the kind of hat worn by a father or a gangster in the old movies. A lemur in a hat—that's what he was.

Hey! the boyfriend yelled. I haven't got all day!

Janice applied her lipstick and blotted her lips on a hanky. Two-tone, she said, pointing at the car, the idea being that two-tone was about as good as it got. Then she climbed into the car without so much as a single backward glance even though everyone knew she was never coming back. It didn't matter that the boyfriend was funny-looking. The important thing was to have a boyfriend. Once you had a boyfriend you were safe—you'd passed the test. Until then everyone was still too young to know for sure.

That was why she told us to look up, someone said. It was a test. It wasn't like there was anything special up there.

I could do it, said someone, tilting her neck by way of demonstration. The night was full of the usual things—a silver moon, some winking stars, a blue-lit scow, the mica-flecked wings of the raptors.

Did you see who couldn't? asked someone else.

I didn't have to see to know, someone said, and it was like everyone knew who she was talking about.

Once you're married you're safe, said someone else. When you're married that means you're really a girl.

I'm never getting married, said the curly-haired girl.

Everyone except her got up and started back home for dinner.

The curly-haired girl stayed on the bench and looked out into the dark seething ocean of park just beyond the sweet yellow tidepool of the street lamp.

All at once she was granted a vision. She saw three things. She saw a lightning bug she wanted to catch but didn't. She saw a flame-colored bird with two sets of wings flying straight up into the air. The higher it flew the more hungry she was for love. She wished for a baseball bat to knock the bird out of the sky; she wished for a baseball cap embroidered with a boy's name in gold. Third, she saw something far away on the other side of the park. The harder she tried to see what it was, the faster she began to move. She could hear the sound of her hooves on turf, moving fast, at a canter.

Little Alton

MISS VICKS HAD BEEN HEADED IN THE SAME DIREC-
tion for a long time now, following the wall. The wall
was about as tall as she was, making it hard for her to see
what was on the other side. Every now and then, though,
she'd get enough of a glimpse to know that the other side
consisted of the same rolling landscape marked at intervals
with the same barbed gray-green shrubs she was forced to
avoid on her own side of the wall, calling the whole point
of the wall into question. The shrubs were century plants—
she'd done a unit on them around the time Mary and Eddie
had been in her classroom. A century plant stayed alive as
long as it took to produce one six-foot-long flower stalk and
then it died. A kindred spirit, Marjorie thought.

She was no longer young but something about the situa-
tion made her feel even older than she was. That much she
knew, that and the fact that she wasn't far from a large body
of water, the sky a shade of blue-violet more usually thought
of as coming from a dactilo port, with handfuls of things
falling loose beneath it that turned out to be seagulls. Every
now and then she was able to catch sight of a tall structure
that seemed like it might be the old water tower she used to
walk past on her way to and from school; it was too far away

to tell, and the base of the structure was hidden under the horizon.

She had discovered the wall only a day or so ago. It was made of stone that had been stuccoed over and whitewashed, and in some places there was a dusty-looking vine growing up it that had cracked the surface, leaving crumbled stucco at its base. The ground was dry and hard-packed and the color of mustard—it was hard to imagine anything thriving under those conditions.

There was something she was supposed to be doing, only she couldn't remember what. She could remember the names of all the students she'd ever taught and she could remember the way her classroom smelled—that was about it. Even in spring with the windows open her classroom smelled like varnish and sour milk. Someone had always thrown up somewhere and then the smell mixed with the smell of the janitor's mop. They were children and they couldn't help it. They couldn't help growing up and becoming adults either.

But this was her *life*, after all. This was the life of Marjorie Vicks, also known as Miss Vicks to the numberless students she had taught, Vicks, M. to the robots, Vicky Dear to the sorcerer. It was her story and she had many ways to tell it, and woe to anyone who tried to say otherwise.

Nor did it make her feel any better to know that everyone was supposed to be doing something—once you reached a certain age that was the way a life was meant to be lived. People who weren't doing anything were sick or insane or babies, though nowadays even the babies had projects. School was out for the summer, so that couldn't be it. But she hadn't been a teacher for years. There had been a retirement party, balloons, presents. It seemed like for some time now she could barely recall what happened from minute to minute, while the distant past was as clear as the Alpine scene in the snow globe that had been a retirement present from one of her students, which as far as she knew was exactly where she'd last seen it, on her coffee table, gathering dust. Or maybe it wasn't. Maybe you left home and it was like the song the girls had been singing right before she rode off on the photographer's horse. The name of the musical the song came from was escaping her—the whole world vanished and everything that had ever been yours vanished with it. Your little dog! But there had been a good reason to leave the dog behind. "And this is what happened," the song said, "the strange thing that happened, to two weary hunters that lost their way."

Not long after she left the street and crossed the vacant lot it had begun raining, lightly at first, a drop here, a drop there, and then heavily, like there wasn't any more air, only rain. The horse moved at a steady pace, the great bellows of its rib cage expanding and contracting between her legs, a feeling she used to love when she was young. The neighborhood changed, rows of houses giving way to shops and the shops to large flat windowless buildings. Gradually the traffic thinned out; the road she was riding on turned to dirt and became narrow, hemmed in on either side by the shapes of tall waving plants. Every now and then there would be a cottage, a mailbox, the glowing eyes of an animal. Marjorie was getting drenched, her suit ruined, and the road was becoming the color of oxblood; her horse was having trouble keeping his footing.

Which way were they headed? She had left in a hurry, without the proper maps. All at once the road took a sharp dip and disappeared under a wide plane of cloudy water. The only way to the other side was by ferryboat, but the ferryman hollered across the water to her that it was a car ferry and she was on a horse.

"I can get off," she hollered back, dismounting.

There was no shelter on her side of the water. On the other

side, overhung by a very large shade tree with something white like a banner or a bedsheet hanging from the low-est bough, there was an open shed in which the ferryman stood, perfectly dry, as he proceeded to set a large engine in motion. He didn't seem to be in much of a hurry. The ferry was like a barge hooked to an underwater cable that drew it back and forth; it, too, seemed to move at a snail's pace, though it probably took no more than five minutes to cross to Marjorie's side of the river.

No one ever melted from standing in the rain, she re-minded herself as she climbed aboard the ferry's unstable deck. She could lift her face to the sky and let the rain wash it the way she used to when she was a girl. Children weren't afraid of rain; they enjoyed getting wet. People didn't al-ways know what they were doing, that much was clear—most people would have known better than to ride away from home on a horse. When Marjorie turned to look back the way she'd come she could see the horse standing on the riverbank, bending his neck to graze, his hide rippling in an involuntary fluid motion like incoming tide. He's better off without me, she thought, and it made her happy to see how delicately his lips moved across the grass.

Once the ferry arrived on the other side she realized that the thing hanging from the tree was an advertisement for a hotel that offered "nightly surprises."

"I don't suppose they're referring to mints on the pillow," Marjorie reflected aloud.

"If they are, I wouldn't eat them," replied the ferryman, taking her hand to help her from the boat and pointing her way to the road, which recommenced at some distance be-hind the shed and could be reached by means of a narrow gravel path that disappeared into a thick clump of bushes.

Marjorie set off with a renewed sense of purpose. Almost immediately the road bent sharply left to follow the same body of water she had just crossed. The distance from shore to shore widened and long narrow islands appeared, shade trees heavy with dark green leaves growing along their banks, black-and-white spotted cows grazing beneath them. On one of the trees she saw another advertisement for the hotel, this one promising "special services." At some point the rain had stopped and a small blurry sun came out, tangled in clouds. A bell began tolling and sections of sky were drifting over the water, making it blue.

It seemed like the road might go on this way forever, following the course of the river—and then all of a sudden, for no apparent reason, it came to an abrupt halt at a high, stuccoed wall. Marjorie looked back and thought she could see the ferry slowly making its way across. Maybe it wasn't the ferry; maybe it was one of those islands and it wasn't moving. She didn't think she was that far from where she'd been when she got off the horse, even though she also felt as if she'd been walking for years. One thing was clear, if she didn't want to go back the way she she'd come she had to leave the road and turn right to follow the wall. The minute she did so the weather changed, taking her completely by surprise. It was exactly like what happened when you opened the oven door to check on whatever was baking inside and a blast of hot air hit you in the face.

Time was either not passing at all or it was passing in one huge lump like a lifetime. The wall showed no sign of coming to an end. Eventually Marjorie got close enough to see that the tower was much bigger than the water tower back home and that it had a flag flying above it. In this latitude everything was lit differently; even when night started to fall everything remained brighter, the sky doing its best to absorb the various colors from the landscape in order to turn itself black.

The flag signified a town, she thought, probably Little

Alton. The word on Little Alton was conflicting. Don't stop there if you can help it. Little Alton's bells were famous. If you stopped in Little Alton you could live forever but then you would also have to stay there forever. Little Alton was beautiful beyond compare. It was heaven on earth; the caravans had been there for such a long time their wheels had sunk into the dirt. They were strung with fairy lights and there were marble plaques planted in their dooryards engraved with the inhabitants' surnames, one of which was bound to be your own.

After a while Marjorie got so close to the tower that she could see that the flag flying above it was red with a gold hand, meaning her assumption that this was Little Alton was correct. The gold hand's fingers were outspread, which meant that the hotel had a vacancy. If she quickened her pace she could make it there before it got any darker.

For some time now she'd been hearing a sound that seemed to be coming from the other side of the wall, a soft padding sound like the paws of a large animal loping across the hardpack. When she stopped, the sound stopped, suggesting that maybe what she was hearing was an echo. The sound was amiable, its absence menacing. A moist wind picked up and she could hear seagulls, the tolling of the bell she'd heard earlier, louder now, like it was inside her ears. It rang four times, though the hour seemed much later. Possibly the number signified something other than time.

She passed a burning haystack on the left, a group of schoolgirls in blue uniforms.

"What happens if you touch it?" one of them was saying.

"You didn't, did you? Did you?"

They gathered to examine the girl's palm.

"See," said another girl. "The part that looks like a burn. That's how you can tell if it was alive or not."

"Well, *was* it?"

"I don't know. It was very cold."

"Like freezer burn?"

"I said I don't know."

The wall continued straight ahead, separating Marjorie from the tower. The girls must have come through some kind of opening, a gate or a door. She was so tired she could barely stay upright. Even so she kept walking. There was no way through the wall, of that she felt positive, just as she knew Little Alton was right there on the opposite side, producing the noise and smells of human interaction, doors opening and closing, wheels moving, motor exhaust, garbage, a hotel. She hadn't seen a scow for a long time, and she wondered whether that meant they didn't come this far north.

A throbbing pain had started up in her left side and she couldn't catch her breath—she had to lie down before she fell. Another large haystack, this one not aflame, seemed to have been erected in her path and she didn't have the energy to walk around it. Instead she slid to the ground and came to rest with her back against the wall. Until she'd arrived here she'd thought she'd been headed north but now she thought she must be facing west, the shrub-strewn landscape unrolling to bunch at the horizon in a line of small irregularly shaped hills capped with tall thin trees, and behind them a spectacular sunset.

She put her cheek to the wall; it felt cool. From the other side came the sound of panting, a rattling chain. Even if she held her breath the sound didn't go away. She made a pillow of her jacket and lay down. The breathing on the other side of the wall grew more regular, eventually turning to gentle snoring, with little growls and yips every now and then. Sometimes it moaned exactly like a man.

"It's all right," Marjorie said. "Shhh."

Often when you thought back you found yourself in an actual moment like it was a place. The rain was falling, long

strings of it breaking loose and hitting the classroom windows. The day was dark, the sky lowering—she'd had to put
on the ceiling lights the moment she got to school. Mary
was sitting at her desk at the front of the room, taking a test.
She was answering questions about the names of Christopher
Columbus's ships. Cutouts of orange and yellow and red
leaves were taped to the windowpanes; Eddie was copying
off Mary's paper. His desk was next to hers and even though
he did this often Miss Vicks never moved him to another
seat. He didn't need Mary's help, she knew that. He only
wanted to share her brain.

He had been a nice-looking boy with delicate fingers like
a concert pianist's, except it was Mary who was the pianist,
albeit a bad one. Eddie had started life uncoordinated and
jumpy and then to everyone's amazement he turned out to
be an athlete. There had been an accident—she strove to remember. Every night all summer long the boys played baseball in the street. From time to time a car would appear.
Not so many cars back then, but even so everyone had to be
careful.

With her back against the wall, Miss Vicks drew her knees
to her chest and tucked her hands under her armpits.

"You can go home now, Edward," she said.

Blue-Eyes

FOR MANY YEARS MARY COULD THINK OF NOTHING EX-
cept her daughter and it was the same for Blue-Eyes—she
couldn't get enough of Mary. She followed her everywhere
with a hand attached to some part of her mother's body or
clothes. Walter wanted to send the girl to a private school
where they learned to speak foreign languages and handle
money and say prayers, but the school was too far away for
Blue-Eyes to attend as a day student, which would have
meant leaving her bed empty night after night with no one
for Mary to read to or sing to sleep. Of course this had been
Walter's plan all along.

Instead Blue-Eyes went to the same school Mary had
gone to, the one just before the first of the three green hills
leading to the Woodard Estate. When she got old enough
Mary dropped her off at the head of the street and Blue-Eyes
walked. She took the same route her mother had taken and,
like her mother, she carried a new schoolbag. Several of the
sycamores had died and been cut down; all of the bubblers
in the schoolyard had been replaced by hygienic drinking
fountains. Mary smelled the plastic of her daughter's schoolbag and felt an ache in her heart, the same ache she felt
when she first held the Yellow Bear. It was a smell associated with those moments when normal time was suspended

and something out of the ordinary happened, like the first game of the spring when a ball landed at her feet and Eddie came running toward her and after he bent to scoop it up his face lifted—so close she could see all his eyelashes sticking out around his eyes like sunbeams in a drawing.

Blue-Eyes loved school, certainly more than Mary, who had preferred naptime and recess. Every Parents' Night the teachers heaped nothing but praise on the girl, and her work was always prominently on display, bearing a gold star or an A+ or 100%. There was something not quite right about Blue-Eyes, though; Mary could see how uncomfortable everything she did made the other parents and the teachers. For example, the movie about the Descent of the Aquanauts that she painted on a roll of shelf paper that got wound on chopstick handles past an opening cut in the bottom of a shoe box—once you started turning the handles it was like you were churning the sea inside the box to such a frenzy it was only a matter of time before it got out and then it would be everywhere, making such a mess you'd never be able to clean it up. "It isn't that your daughter can't do the work," the teachers said, peering earnestly into Mary's face. "She can do everything, but . . ." They were never able to finish the sentence, a problem Mary had long since grown used to.

Teachers came and teachers went but the school itself remained remarkably unchanged. Strips of Palmer method script still hung above the chalkboards, and the same lifeless tortoise still kept guard outside the principal's office. The sombrous mural in hues of brown showing soldiers planting a flag on a hill was still hanging in the same place it had been hanging the time Mary found Eddie standing in the hallway after they'd been told he was never coming back, and there he was, the same as ever. "I have something I want to tell you," he said, but then the fire drill bell went off and she never got to hear what he had to say.

At some point everyone who had ever known you, including much younger people, would forget you and die without ever having told people even younger than themselves about you—and then you would really be *gone*. Miss Vicks had had a love story, but who could remember it? It was said Miss Vicks, herself, remembered nothing. Mary hit Eddie on the head with her wand to get his attention when they were in some play together but all that happened was he got a bloody nose afterward. If you wanted to be remembered you had to become famous—that was the lesson history taught you, if you chose to pay attention to it. Even so, the person you'd been, the person who breathed and had blood circulating through every part of herself, would be gone.

"It's different for some people," Downie told Mary. "Ever since that night on the street, blood is no longer part of the story for Eddie."

"What do you mean?" she asked.

She had taken to visiting number 37 in the afternoons before Blue-Eyes got home from school and while Walter was still at work. She liked returning to the street now that she no longer lived there. The robots' house felt different; the love seat and the television set had disappeared but even so the house felt less empty than it had when she was a girl, chiefly due to the fact that all of the apparently empty space in it was filled by Downie. He'd told her this, otherwise she wouldn't have known. Whenever she came to visit he assumed a smaller, hospitable form, more like a man, really, though the house had a smell to it that made her think of the places where animals lived, one combining damp fur and urine and earth.

"I very much doubt whether Eddie still sees in color,"

Downie continued. "He can see a lot. He can see everything a person needs to see in order to play baseball. But that doesn't mean he has a heart."

Mary looked through the bay window. If she ignored the way some of the trees were gone and some of the others were so huge she couldn't see their tops it was almost like nothing had changed at all. The inside of the house was cold, as cold as Downie himself. "He's good to his parents," she said. "He always sends them money."

"He got what he asked for," Downie reminded her.

They were sitting in the living room at the kitchen table, which Mary was sure only appeared for her benefit. Downie had made her an egg salad sandwich, sliced on the diagonal, the way he knew she preferred it.

"Whatever Eddie asked for," Mary said, "it certainly wasn't me."

"He got baseball," Downie said. "You got what you wanted, too." His voice was like ice and Mary knew he meant Blue-Eyes. "You would do anything for her," Downie said. "Remember?"

"That was a long time ago," Mary said.

"You must remember the sound the hare made when you ran over it," Downie persisted. "It isn't often a person gets to hear a sound like that."

"I do remember," Mary said; she knew she would never forget the horror she'd felt that night in the clearing.

As for Blue-Eyes, after five thousand days it was as if Mary and her daughter had never known one another. Mary sang "There is a tavern in the town." She read "The Hullocks were blackening as Velvet cantered down the chalk road to the village." Blue-Eyes put her fingers in her ears. Mary's smallest mistakes incensed her—like when she called the store Penneys and not JCPenney, as if it were the height of hypocrisy for an adult to pretend to know anything and get something as simple as that wrong.

Meanwhile the sorcerer was happy to have his wife back. Mary lifted her hips to him; her eyes clicked into their sockets like a doll's eyes on stems. He found a paw print filled with rainwater in the rose bed and drank it, greedily, in gratitude.

With every passing year Blue-Eyes became prettier and harder to get along with. By her fifteenth birthday Mary had had enough.

"Where is that brochure?" she asked.

St. Foy was run by an order of sisters dedicated to silence and good works and turning even very difficult girls into model citizens. The saint herself had been deemed sweeter and more fragrant than honeycomb; she was twelve years old when she died. The brochure showed her standing atop a pedestal, her head piled high with snow. In the brochure it described how it was snow that had come to the saint's aid when she was undergoing her martyrdom on a red-hot grill, veiling her body from the curious eyes of onlookers. On the other hand, suspicions about the place abounded. For one thing, snow never fell there, it being on the coast. For another, Foy was said to be a perversion of Fée, which was French for "fairy," a fact you'd figure out soon enough in one of the language classes.

To Mary's surprise, Blue-Eyes raised no objection to the plan. "When you were born," Mary said, "I loved you so much I never wanted to let you go."

"Born, Mother?" Blue-Eyes said. She was holding a round plaid suitcase in one hand and tapping at the side of her head with the other, trying to disable the port without Mary noticing. A rectangular plaid suitcase stood between them. Her father had given Blue-Eyes the set of matching luggage

for her fifteenth birthday, the anniversary of his collision
with the Yellow Bear. "I get the message," she said as she
tore off the wrapping paper.

On the drive to St. Foy there had been no wind but when
they arrived at the school's imposing front entrance the
wind began to blow off the ocean. Dead leaves and shade
poured from the hydrangea bushes on either side of the door.
The seabirds grew mute; Mary rang the bell. The door was
a single wood plank without a window. There was no window since whoever opened the door wasn't supposed to have
to look first to see who was out there. As Mary was well
aware, even the most disgraced of God's creatures was welcome in a convent.

Given the exorbitant tuition, as Walter had pointed out
to her, the nuns didn't really need to worry. He had stayed
behind, having been forewarned in a dream not to go. In the
dream he stepped from his silver-gray car and into a pool of
shadows. Just like in real life, the wind was blowing off the
ocean and the seabirds were silent. The road went uphill and
down and was called a *scaletta*, meaning staircase but also
skeleton. As long as his skeleton didn't have a soul in it he
would be welcome there. A sorcerer with a soul, though—
that was another matter.

"Just wait here," said the young woman with frizzy black
hair who opened the door. She turned her back on Mary and
Blue-Eyes and took off down a long dark hallway.

The vestibule was square and forest green. With the front
door closed it was every bit as dark as the hall. A mahogany
table stood to the left, a porcelain umbrella stand containing several umbrellas and a pair of crutches to the right; the
hallway down which the young woman disappeared extended straight ahead, ending in a set of swinging doors.
From behind the swinging doors came the sound of running water, chair legs moving on wood, high-pitched girlish

voices; closer at hand, maybe on the other side of the wall, someone opened what seemed to be a closet door and began rummaging around, rattling hangers.

The young woman never returned. In her stead a very old woman with big watery eyes appeared, pushing a walker ahead of herself. "Say good-bye to your mother," the old woman said and averted her gaze as if from the sight of something distasteful. The vestibule used to be wallpapered with pink flowers, Mary remembered, just as she knew the old woman hadn't always needed to use a walker. Though she was dressed in a black habit and a white headdress she didn't look much like a nun, and it wasn't just because of the fact that she wasn't wearing a cross.

"Good-bye, Mother," Blue-Eyes said, tipping her cheek in Mary's direction for a kiss.

"I'm not going anywhere until you say you love me," Mary said. Out of the corner of her eye she caught a glimpse of a flickering curtain of light just above the umbrella stand. This could mean her age was catching up with her and her cornea was coming loose or it could mean there was actually something there.

"I love you, Mother," Blue-Eyes said, but she didn't sound convincing. She, too, was looking in the direction of the wall above the umbrella stand. "Tell Dad he did the right thing," she said. "Not coming."

"He wanted to come," Mary said, "but he had work to do."

Blue-Eyes turned to face her. "He would have died," she said, and when Mary laughed she shook her head. "For real," she said. "Dad would have died for real. Don't you understand anything?" She returned her attention to the wall.

"It's time for you to leave," the old woman told Mary. She maneuvered her walker around so that it faced the empty hallway, then she looked back over her shoulder. "As for you, young lady," she said, "it's time for you to come inside."

Blue-Eyes followed the old woman down the hallway. It seemed to go on forever but eventually they arrived at an elevator. "I'm the only one allowed to operate this," the old woman told her. It was the kind of elevator where you pulled open a brass gate and slid a heavy lever in place before you could get it to move. "The girls are at dinner," the old woman said. The elevator began to ascend in small jerks like a Ferris wheel. "You can join them after you get settled in."

Blue-Eyes's room was about the same size and shape as the vestibule. The only difference was that it had a window facing the water; in the morning she would have a good view of the sun coming up above the still-dark strand. The room contained a narrow bed and a dresser; there was a thick layer of dust on the baseboards and the empty bodies of horseflies and June bugs in the space between the storm and interior windows. The old woman told Blue-Eyes the last girl who'd stayed in the room had died in it; she choked on a saltine after refusing to do as she was told.

Folded at the foot of the bed was a set of long underwear with a note pinned to it explaining that in the interest of saving money the building was kept unheated. Blue-Eyes had no need for long underwear but how was the school expected to know that? She put the clothes she'd brought with her away in the dresser and sat on the bed—the mattress was thin and seemed to be stuffed with straw, but otherwise wasn't too bad. Oddly, this was one form of comfort she'd found she couldn't do without.

Somewhere nearby the sound of singing started. Blue-Eyes left her room and followed the sound until she came to a wide landing at the head of a formal staircase, the newel posts topped with tense-looking creatures with wings, supposed to look like angels. If you stared at them long enough though—just as she'd done with the flickering curtain of light in the vestibule—you could see the wings twitching, the eyes shifting this way and that. Brightness poured up the staircase from below but not high enough to reach the landing. The old woman with the walker stood at the far side of it, beckoning to Blue-Eyes to hurry up.

Inside the chapel there were girls of all ages and sizes, not arranged in any obvious order, all of them wearing sky-blue uniforms. Blue-Eyes slid into an empty pew near the back. The service was a mystery to her; she'd never been in a place like this before, and the book she'd been handed at the door was crammed full of different-colored bookmarks. At some point the girl with frizzy dark hair who'd opened the front door for them slipped into the pew behind her and tapped her on the shoulder. "Come to my room after," she said, handing Blue-Eyes a piece of paper with her name and room number written on it. She was called Penny, which made sense, since her face was round and her features in faint relief like on a coin.

The service seemed as though it would never end. Finally a nun got up to snuff the candles, releasing a thread of smoke straight from each wick. The smell was sweet, the candles—as Blue-Eyes knew from reading the brochure—a product of the school's own honeycombs. One by one the sisters filed through a side door, the ones who were able bending a knee to bow deeply before the altar. The girls went out the same door they'd come in through in a disorderly crowd. No one was talking to anyone else. That was the rule: you had to keep silent all night long until after breakfast.

The later it got the harder the wind began to blow, rattling the windows. The school buildings were set high on a hill and were very old. At one time they'd been painted white but now they looked almost silver. Every night the wind came pawing at them, taking their paint away bit by bit, filling the night with particles. Everything vulnerable was on the move, dropping shadows. The light got blocked the way it always did at night, letting people sleep.

Back home Mary tried contacting her daughter but the receptor wasn't working. Blue-Eyes did this all the time—it was nothing new. She would put things in the port the way children put jelly beans up their nose, the difference being that it didn't result in a trip to the doctor and it cost a fortune to fix.

Walter was at a meeting; he wouldn't be home until much later. When he stayed out late like this, Mary had no idea when he got in. The next morning he would be sitting at the kitchen table in his plaid bathrobe with nothing on underneath, reading the newspaper and drinking coffee like a normal husband. There would be a pile of defrosted waffles on his plate but Mary was pretty sure they were only there for show, as if to provide the illusion that he was having a regular breakfast. The eyes of the cat in the clock that used to belong to her parents would jerk from side to side and he would give the paper a little shake. This was a signal for Mary to untie the sash and let the two halves of his robe fall away, revealing his erect phallus. She could straddle it or take it in her mouth—the choice was hers. When she was finished he would keep her coming with his fingers. Sex with him was never disappointing the way it used to be with Eddie, but she figured that was because she couldn't ever forget it was Eddie she was having sex with, making it harder for her to completely lose herself in the act.

Mary tried Blue-Eyes one more time; the receptor still wasn't operational. The house felt especially empty and the dark sky out the picture window seemed oddly loose like fabric there was too much of. Please don't let this be happening, she thought. When Walter said what he did about Space Drift that night in his apartment she'd thought it was one of those things like the Rain of Beads that had happened a long time ago and would never happen again.

Never again, Mary thought. She sat down at her sewing machine and began attaching the waistband to the skirt she hadn't finished making in time for Blue-Eyes to take it with her to school. As she sat there the moon appeared in the picture window. It was close to full but not quite— nothing out of the ordinary in the way of a moon but beautiful nonetheless.

Whatever she had felt for Eddie—and, really, she wasn't sure what that had been, only that it had been everything for her—she chalked up to the fires of youth, which she told herself were behind her. She was encouraged to feel this way, to belittle everything that had happened between her and Eddie. Time healed all wounds, everyone knew that, just as they knew the moon was a rock and nothing more. It came out of the place where the Pacific Ocean was now; a monkey had landed there and then people had walked on it. She would get over feeling sad about Blue-Eyes, too, but not immediately. For the moment she preferred to feel sad.

Mary bit off the thread and held up the skirt. The school had provided the pattern and the finished garment was surprisingly unattractive; she couldn't imagine her daughter consenting to wear such a thing. She dropped it on the floor. Tomorrow, she thought. Tomorrow I'll put it in the mail. Then she walked to the piano and pulled out the bench and sat on it. The moon is a rock, Mary thought, but you could see how it loved the place it came from in the way it wouldn't let go of the tides. The moon loved water. Whereas water had a more complicated relationship with rock—without rock, the water could be everywhere. Mary opened her port all the way and began to play the *Moonlight Sonata*. She had never been any good, she knew that, but she also knew this piece by heart. The further into it she got, the louder she played.

At some point she saw a light go on in the nearest neighbor's house. The nearest neighbor was too far away and too shielded by massive plantings of ornamental shrubbery and shade trees to be able to hear Mary play. Then again, she was using the pedal and had the lid propped open.

PENNY AND BLUE-EYES WERE KNEELING BY THE FIRE IN Penny's room; they were toasting crumpets the way young men did in the leather-bound books about school life in England. In the books, as at St. Foy, one young person's future was always going to turn out better than the other's.

"What's that?" Penny asked, cocking her head.

Penny was an "old girl"—she'd lived at St. Foy for as long as she could remember. Her room was about four times the size of Blue-Eyes's and had a fireplace, a sitting area with a camelback love seat upholstered in gold velvet, a four-poster canopy bed, and a Queen Anne highboy. Penny also had an aquarium containing a small pink castle and a large brown fish that stuck itself to the side of the tank with its mouth. Pets were against the rules at St. Foy, but Penny, as she'd told Blue-Eyes, was a rule breaker.

"What's what?" Blue-Eyes asked, oblivious to the music leaking from her port. The problem with jamming the apparatus the way she did was that you could do it once too often and then you couldn't make it stay shut ever again.

"Let's get something straight," Penny said. "If you keep pretending not to know what I'm talking about like that, out the door you go. No!" Penny added, and she sounded angry. "That is *exactly* what I mean. That sad expression. Like you're a poor little orphan girl."

"It's my mother," Blue-Eyes admitted. She had been puzzled, not sad, and was surprised by Penny's outburst. It wasn't in Blue-Eyes's nature to pretend anything.

"Your *mother* is a poor little orphan girl?"

"No, my mother is the one who is playing the piano."

"Turn it up," Penny said. "Is that really her playing? Your mother can play the piano?"

"She's trying to make me feel bad."

"Why would she do that?" Penny asked. "She's your *mother*. Doesn't she love you?"

"She does," Blue-Eyes said. "That's the whole problem."

Her mother owned a highboy like the one in Penny's room—it had come to her along with the cat clock and the many other articles of furniture she inherited when her parents got divorced. This was what her mother's life was like, Blue-Eyes thought, a large piece of furniture where almost all the drawers held no surprises except for the least reachable top middle drawer—the one with a cockle shell carved in the wood—which was filled to the brim with things Blue-Eyes never saw her mother wear and knew she never would, white cotton underpants, shoes with stiletto heels, a fancy pink prom dress, a broken pair of eyeglasses.

Penny yanked Blue-Eyes's hair back from the port and rested her ear against the hole, letting the music pour out of it and into her head. "Lucky you," she said. "If I had a mother like yours I'd be the happiest girl alive."

Number 24

EVEN AFTER THEIR SON BECAME FAMOUS AND BEGAN sending them money, Eddie's parents remained on the street. Most of the people who'd been living there when he was a boy had moved away, some of them into fancier houses, some of them into retirement communities or nursing homes, some of them into the ground. Of the original families only the Darlings and Mr. O'Toole and Carol XA remained. Mary's parents had gone their separate ways years earlier, Mrs. O'Toole died the year the street became infested with insects so small they could fly through anything, the Duffys moved to be closer to Roy and Cindy and the grandchildren. Aside from the photographer, no one knew where Miss Vicks had been going when she left, though everyone registered her absence. She didn't really have any friends, yet the street felt empty without her and her little red dog. They were more reliable than a clock for telling time.

One night not long after Miss Vicks disappeared, Carol XA overheard a whining noise coming from inside number 49 as she was flying past the porch. When she went inside she found the dog sitting in the middle of the living room carpet, obviously hungry but otherwise none the worse for wear. Carol took him home with her to number 37.

Pet care didn't come naturally to the robots—they found

it difficult to fathom the relationship between humans and animals. Sometimes we befriended them, sometimes we made things out of them like shoes or belts, often we ate them. Occasionally humans took the form of animals and when this happened they were always kinder than regular human beings.

Carol copied Miss Vicks's practice of "taking the dog for a walk." She enjoyed the slow, stately rhythm dog walking induced in her mechanism, the ritual pause, the insertion of her hand into the plastic bag, the stooping down and the scooping up, the tying of the knot and the ultimate disposal of the neat little bundle. Because she had no sense of smell there was nothing unpleasant about the transaction. All the inhabitants of number 37 liked to make the dog do tricks but it was Carol who truly seemed to love the creature. She could be seen petting its sleek russet head, nipping her front teeth together in involuntary expressions of tenderness exactly like Miss Vicks used to do.

Miss Vicks's leaving was a blessing in disguise—that was the general opinion of everyone on the street. Having a pet made the robots more human, which in turn brought out the best in the humans. Mrs. Darling knit the dog a long green sweater. Mr. O'Toole never left home without a pocket full of treats. Eddie's father made sure there was a bowl of fresh water on the sidewalk by the foot of the front steps at all times. As for the robots, they knew Miss Vicks was never coming back.

Eddie's parents had stayed on the street because his mother wanted to be in the same place if her boy returned, either as a person or a spirit, she didn't care which as long as she got to see him again. His father had already reserved a space for himself and his wife in the new retirement community that was said to be going up where the Woodard Estate used to stand. In the meantime he busied himself maintaining the lawn. It took almost every ounce of his energy to push the mower up the hill and then make sure it didn't get away from him going back down. Everyone else on the street had abandoned the idea of having a lawn, paving over the grass or adding an extension that displaced the yard completely. Many of the new people were young families with children, not unlike the way it had been when Eddie was a boy, though the children were different, less apt to play outdoors.

Maintaining the front lawn had become a point of pride with Eddie's father, who wanted to set an example for the young families, to show them that just because the world often seemed to reward ugliness was no excuse to give up on beauty. Granted, the ivy plant in the Italian cachepot on the bow-window sill was no longer a living thing but made of plastic. The lawn was mostly stringweed, mowed to look like grass. When it got cut it didn't smell sweet like grass, either. It smelled fishy, similar to algae.

The day was becoming hot, the sky like an open mouth, and the heat had a broad sucking quality no one could get used to. Eddie's father had almost finished mowing and was standing on the sidewalk, using his large white handkerchief to wipe the sweat from his bright-red face. The sycamore in front of their house was one of the ones that had sickened and died and been chopped down. In its place the community association had planted something that looked more like a twig. The street used to be so shady, even during the hottest months. No wonder the children stayed inside now.

Eddie's mother stayed inside too. She claimed the sun made her feel faint, though everyone agreed she'd been a different person ever since Eddie had gone on the DL and hadn't come back. Saturday night Eddie's father still frequented the Venetian Club and once he'd had enough to drink could be persuaded to take the baton and lead the band for a number or two. Eddie's mother used to be one of the best dancers on the floor; everyone said Eddie got his fleetness of foot, his animal grace, from her. He looked like her too, with his thick dark hair and full lips, but he got his hazel eyes and tender spirit from his father.

"I'm waiting," Eddie's mother yelled through the open front door. Like most of the older people on the street they still felt safe using screens, having built up immunity during the year of the infestation. "The ice cubes are melting."

"I'll be right there," Eddie's father yelled back. "I'm almost done."

He was watching the approach from the far end of the street of Carol XA, who had stopped at the corner to let her dog sniff the holly bush. Ever since she'd adopted Miss Vicks's dog, Carol had adopted her habits and mannerisms as well, wearing sweater sets and tweed suits and playing the part of the perfect spinster. Unlike her predecessor, though, she always had a ready store of neighborhood gossip. Eddie's father enjoyed passing the time of day with her.

"Lunch is ready *now!*" Eddie's mother yelled.

If her husband didn't come in soon she would have to eat both sandwiches herself, something she did more and more frequently, contributing to a growing weight problem. She used to be lithe, like Eddie; in a form-fitting gown she could steal a man's breath away and fill a woman's soul with envy. At least now that she was fat she had some friends. Plus the sandwiches were her favorite, sea legs mixed with mayonnaise and celery—to slow herself down she cut them into quarters. A small gray-brown bird she'd never seen before settled on the bird feeder outside the kitchen window, fluffed its feathers, and then made itself smooth again, looking her in the eye.

It was as if she was supposed to do something, though she didn't know what. For want of anything better she activated the console, a miniature one built into the wall above the kitchen counter for times like this, when her craving for human company was overpowering. The reception was poor, but what she thought was static turned out to be the noise of an overexcited crowd. ". . . a stunning development, Bob," the sportscaster was saying, "absolutely stunning. I don't think anyone saw this coming . . ."

The picture shifted to the ball field, where a player wearing Rockets jersey number 24 was sliding into home plate. He looked young and strong, exactly the way he'd looked the day he collided with his teammate in front of the Alka-Seltzer sign. It was hard to see anything clearly, though; the picture was fuzzy and because the sun was in his face he was wearing twin patches of black paint under his eyes. Eddie's mother sat on the kitchen floor, her appetite knocked out of her. "Back to you, Heidi," the sportscaster said.

The crowd kept cheering, a sea of paper bag–colored faces with little holes for mouths. When they started singing "Take Me Out to the Ball Game," Eddie's signature tune, the picture switched to the owner's box, where the owner was making a victory sign with his fingers while his wife sat beside him stiff as a board in a white linen dress and a black straw hat with an unusually wide brim. It was impossible to see her expression—when the crowd got to "I don't care if I never get back" the camera pulled in for a close-up, whereupon she gripped both knees with her white-gloved hands and put her head in her lap.

Eddie's mother thought the owner's wife looked like she was going to be sick and she felt no sympathy. Of course she'd never heard the real story; as far as she was concerned, if it hadn't been for Mary, Eddie would still be here. It was hard to remember that there had been a time when the future seemed so certain it was as if it had already happened and it was possible to summon even the smallest details of it as if they were distant memories: the four of them eating lunch at the card table in the living room, the sunlight sliding through the bow window in a great yellow block the way it always did at midday. Make that five and put them in the dining room along with a high chair, an entire family shuttling around and through the sun, dragging their shadows behind them like trains. Her granddaughter was a sly little monkey, dark-haired like her daddy. The child didn't always want to try something new like sea-leg sandwiches, but Grammy had her ways. Then they all played cards.

"I'm feeling good," Eddie was telling Heidi. The Rockets had won the playoffs with Eddie's grand slam home run in the game's final at bat. He didn't look any different than he had the last time his mother saw him—he had a pleasant face but rarely did he smile. The last time she saw him— when could that have been? As crystal clear as the future once seemed, the past now seemed cloaked in mystery. So much time had gone by. New people had moved onto the street, most of them nice enough but total strangers. Mr. Costello sold his haberdashery to a chain. The trolley barn had become a walk-in clinic.

Meanwhile Eddie's father had finished mowing the grass verge in front of number 24 and was turning to greet Carol XA.

"Looks like someone's thirsty," he said, moving the water bowl closer to her little dog who was straining at the leash.

"You do such a beautiful job," Carol said. She stood looking back the way she'd come, blinking her eyes rapidly the way a robot does when agitated. "I only wish everyone took as much care with their property."

"It isn't easy," Eddie's father said. He knew she was talking about Mr. O'Toole, who had let things go since his wife died. Even though the ornamental shrubbery in front of their house was plastic it had shed most of its leaves, and the paint had peeled from all their window and door frames. "Sometimes life throws us curves," he added.

For several moments they both stood without saying a word, watching while the dog lapped up water. At last Carol pulled a balled tissue from the sleeve of her cardigan and began to dab at her eyes. "They seemed like such a devoted couple," she said with a sigh.

All at once, as it had many times before, the long silver-gray car approached from the far end of the street, moving fast. Because of the missing trees the sun reflected directly off the car's hood, turning it to a blaze of light almost as hard to look at as the face of the sun itself.

"Keep back!" Carol said, handing Eddie's father the leash. Already she was moving too fast to register the moment when the leash slipped from his fingers—before anyone could stop her she had stepped off the curb directly into the path of the speeding car.

It was like watching a bright thing intersect with a thing even brighter, neither system's mechanics even remotely compatible with the usual thermodynamic laws. Once again there was the sound of squealing brakes, a soft thump. Then the car's rear door opened, letting Eddie out. He stumbled to regain balance and began walking unsteadily, listing from side to side.

"They shouldn't have let you leave the hospital before you were ready," Carol said. She was standing back on the sidewalk, Miss Vicks's dog lying in the gutter at her feet.

"What hospital? I was never in any hospital," Eddie replied. "Besides, no one told me not to leave."

"That should have gone without saying."

As the car continued speeding toward the Avenue, Eddie's mother caught a glimpse of Mary through the passenger window. She looked older—not *old*, but not young, either—

sitting there blowing her nose while her husband's long fingers deftly wormed their way around behind her bent neck to come out the other side and pat her on the shoulder. Maybe it was that she seemed less vibrant, less hopeful, though that may have had less to do with aging than with the way she was living her life now that Blue-Eyes had been sent away to school. Eddie's father had told her he was pretty sure he'd seen Mary walking near the former trolley barn in the direction of the Mermaid Tavern. She was always nicely dressed but seemed to have trouble staying upright—following in her mother's footsteps, you might say. Women often got the tips of their high heels caught in the trolley tracks.

"Didn't anyone hear me?" Eddie's mother asked. She had come onto the porch when she heard the brakes and now she couldn't believe her eyes. Her husband was standing on the grass verge, hugging a person who looked exactly like her son. "Lunch is ready," she said.

Meanwhile Carol XA stood there cradling the limp russet body of Miss Vicks's dog in her arms. Of course the robots were aware of the fact that all living beings experienced a thing called "death," but none of them had ever given much thought to what being dead actually meant. No one heard the sound the robot was making as the car arrived at the Avenue and turned right; it wasn't coming from Carol but from somewhere far away that also seemed like it was inside her mouth. I don't think she'd known what would happen when she stopped the car, only that it was her job to get Eddie out of it.

"You're looking good," said Eddie's father.

"Thanks, Dad," Eddie said.

Inside number 24 the card table had been set for two. With Eddie's help his mother added a third setting, summoning as she did the future she so ardently desired. Together she and Eddie arranged the sea-leg sandwiches on the blue willow plates, poured iced tea into the jelly glasses, and folded the napkins.

"It's good to have you home, son," Eddie's father said, shaking the napkin back into a square and inserting it in his shirt collar like a bib.

"It's good to be home," Eddie replied. He said it to be polite, but as soon as the words left his mouth he realized it was the truth. In a way it was like he'd never left. After lunch he and Mary would walk back to school together. Miss Vicks would be at the blackboard, writing yet another problem in long division.

"How is Miss Vicks, anyway?" he asked, and his mother looked down at her sandwich.

"She died," Eddie's father said. "We thought you knew."

"She hadn't been well," said Eddie's mother. "She hadn't been well for a long time. That photographer from the paper took some cute shots of her posing on that horse of his—I think he was the last person to see her before she went. The paper used one of them for the obituary. I've kept it around here somewhere in case you wanted to see it."

"That's OK, Mom," Eddie said, putting a hand on her shoulder to make her sit back in her chair. "You can look for it later." He took a sip of his iced tea and frowned. "The thing is," he said, "I could have sworn I heard her talking to me the other night. Not all that long ago, either."

"If anyone was going to return as a ghost, it would be Marjorie Vicks," Eddie's father said, but Eddie shook his head.

"It was *her*," he said. "She told me I ought to come home." He looked puzzled. "She told me to come home and here I am."

Undaunted, the sun came swimming through the bow window; as if on cue they all lifted a sandwich quarter from their plates.

"Well, however it happened, we're glad you're here," said Eddie's mother. She was watching to see whether he would eat the sandwich. The sea-legs looked like they came from a crab, but she was pretty sure they'd been produced in a factory. "You're a grown man. You've got a life of your own to live now." What she was thinking was "if you're actually alive to live it" only she didn't dare say it aloud.

The grandfather clock in the corner began playing the Westminster chimes just as it always used to, except out of phase. Eddie used to be afraid of the face on the moon that appeared in the upper part of the dial when the real moon outside became full. Let's go upstairs and get away from *that*, he'd whisper to Mary—that was how he first got to touch her breasts. They'd been quite small and perfectly hemispheric like teacups. Remember that time in assembly? she'd asked. When you were Mr. Robin and I was Miss Springtime and I forgot my line and you said it for me? Wake up, Mr. Robin! And then I hit you on the head with my wand.

"Actually," Eddie said. "I'd like to move back into my old room if it's all the same to everyone." From where he sat he had a view of the first few steps leading to the second floor. His room had been at the head of the stairs and from his bed he and Mary were able to see into the backyard. He knew without looking that the climbing roses were in bloom.

"You wouldn't recognize it," his father said. "Your mother took it over years ago."

"He snores," his mother explained. "I could never get any sleep."

"Of course you need your sleep," Eddie said. He patted his lips with his napkin, though he hadn't had a bite to eat.

"Everyone needs sleep," Eddie's father said. "Even a famous ballplayer like you."

Eddie began to get up from the table. "You're right," he

said, and he realized he had never felt so tired in his life. "There's a big game tomorrow. I ought to be getting to bed."

The sandwiches had all been eaten; the juice glasses were empty. Outside it was pitch black. "My goodness," said Eddie's father. "Where has the time gone?"

The grandfather clock started to strike but no one was counting.

His mother began clearing dishes, talking softly to herself. "Speaking of time," she said. "One night, a long time ago, you were late coming home. Do you remember?"

It was all his father could do to keep from crying. "We tried to do our best, Eddie," he said. He was scrubbing away at a place on the surface of the card table, scrubbing and scrubbing as if there were a spot there even though Eddie couldn't see anything. "We never knew what happened."

"I sold my soul," Eddie said. "I sold my soul to the sorcerer. And this is what I got in return."

The Bardo

IF SHE'D ONLY GONE A FEW STEPS FARTHER THE NIGHT before, Marjorie Vicks would have ended up at the back entrance to the Seaview Hotel. The door there had once been bright blue and was built into the wall she'd fallen asleep against, the hotel's name stenciled in gold across the top of a single small window above the tiny gold image of an anchor. While she slept the weather had taken a turn for the worse. She arose feeling stiff and chilled through; a heavy dew had fallen, leaving her clothes thick and wet, the fate, as she had come to understand, of all women who ran away from home.

A hallway filled with garbage led to the hotel kitchen. The kitchen was empty, a kettle on the verge of whistling on the stove. From the floor above came the sound of someone running a vacuum cleaner. She tried calling "hello" but her lips were stiff and she had trouble forming the word.

She removed her wet jacket. It was warm in the kitchen and something sweet was baking in the oven. When no one answered she pushed through another, brighter blue door in the wall opposite and found herself in the hotel dining room. The room was spacious with four tall windows providing a view of the sea; sitting at one of the window tables was a young girl dressed like the schoolgirls Marjorie had seen outside just before falling asleep. The girl sat slouched over the table, her head propped in one hand, looking toward the water.

"Hello," Marjorie said again, this time managing to make herself heard.

The girl turned to face her. She had a very round face and an abundance of dark hair like uncarded wool. "Care to join us?" she asked, indicating a chair adjacent to her own. Despite her use of first person plural and the fact that the table seemed to have been set for three, with knives and forks and spoons and flowered dessert plates, there was no one else in sight. "If you want anything to eat in this place you have to get it yourself." The girl pointed in the direction of the bright blue door, behind which the kettle suddenly stopped whistling.

Marjorie hesitated. During the night she seemed to have turned to a block of ice and the dining room was even warmer than the kitchen. In her condition, the heat might prove dangerous.

The girl studied her face, moving her eyes across different parts of it like someone scanning a landscape. "Everybody has to eat," she said.

It was ten o'clock in the morning—Marjorie had slept late. The tide had reached its lowest ebb a half hour earlier, laying the beach bare. She could see a brown shoe and a carburetor and a great many piles of seashells and seaweed and dead sea creatures. At some point she realized her teeth were chattering but she couldn't tell if it was because she was chilled to the bone or because something about her table companion was making her nervous. "Maybe just a cup of tea," she said, and the next thing she knew the girl had leapt up and disappeared into the kitchen.

She returned carrying two large white take-out cups with lids. "The hotel management is using teabags now," she warned. She introduced herself as Penny. When she first came here, Penny said, there had been fresh flowers at every table and an attentive waitstaff. Now the flowers were plastic and the management used paper placemats instead of lace tablecloths. The hummingbird feeders were still there, attached to the windows with suction cups, but the hummingbirds had been replaced by large moths that arrived at dusk.

How did I get here? Marjorie wondered. It had been a night in summer. There had been a horse and a ferryboat. Later there was a wall and later still there was an animal that might have been a dog. A big dog though, nothing like her own little pet. She could hear the sound the dog's nails made as it ran along beside her on the other side of the wall. She could hear the rattling of its collar.

"What about those 'special services' I saw advertised?" she asked, suddenly remembering the white sheet hanging from the limb of a large tree. "Is the hotel management still making them available?" The tea was lukewarm and had a lot of milk and sugar in it. Even so, it tasted delicious.

"That depends." Penny leaned back in her chair, lifting her thicket of hair in one clump and positioning it firmly behind her. "Some people find them desirable, others not so much. Are you planning to stay the night? You should, you know," she said. "The rooms are delightful, especially the corner suites with balconies."

"I'm afraid I can't," Marjorie replied.

"A lot of parents stay over," Penny said. "Those with girls at the school, that is." She took a sip from her cup and made a face. "It's amazing how fast tea loses heat in these cups."

People used to say that being a teacher was like being the mother of thousands but Marjorie knew that wasn't true. Even the students she'd felt a special attachment to had left her classroom without a single backward glance. They were differently composed, elusive as minnows. "I'm not a parent," she admitted shyly, finishing her tea and returning the cup to the table. But what exactly *am* I then? she wondered.

Time was making a ticking sound as it passed though there didn't seem to be a clock anywhere in sight. A vision came to Marjorie of her dog trotting around inside the house, looking for something to eat. Every so often she would forget to fill his water bowl and, small as he was, he would end up drinking from the toilet. She saw him lying on the floor beside the refrigerator with his tongue hanging out like a piece of lunch meat. I'm a dog owner, she thought, that's what I am. The thing about a vision was it didn't let you zoom in to see whether your dog had stopped breathing. The ticking was coming from an oven timer, but Marjorie couldn't tell if it was in the hotel kitchen or part of the vision. Seconds were always passing this way, thimbleful by thimbleful, as were the lives of living beings. This was why you kept getting smaller as you got older; it had nothing to do with bone loss.

Above their heads the vacuum cleaner suddenly stopped; a door banged shut.

Penny looked up at the ceiling. "It sounds like you're in luck," she said. "If you change your mind and decide you want a room, that is."

Marjorie was surprised at how relieved she felt to see Penny tilt her neck. It was ridiculous, she thought, how the old superstitions refused to die. The Horsewomen! Girls of a certain age still managed to have this effect, just as there were still women who claimed to be descended from them—chiefly nurses, a few actresses. In most cases it wasn't clear if the girls making these claims were looking for praise or pity, like the ones who insisted they cast no shadow. Many families had a photograph of a shadowless female relative tucked away in a drawer somewhere.

"I only dropped in," Marjorie explained. "I wasn't planning to stay. I didn't even bring my purse."

"That's what they all say," Penny said, letting out a sigh.

Just then the tide began to come in. It came pouring onto the beach all at once, filled with fish and who knew what else. If there was a name for this phenomenon Marjorie had forgotten it. A gull sailed past the window and landed atop the carburetor just before the carburetor disappeared under the water and the gull took off. Why did gulls always show themselves in profile, she wondered, never head-on?

Meanwhile Penny began fidgeting with her hair, scooping it up and lowering it, the expression on her face difficult to read. Suddenly she smiled. "Well, look who's finally decided to join us," she said, pointing in the direction of the window.

Marjorie turned in her seat but all she could see was the water advancing toward them. The waves had a wild, disorganized appearance, black and green-black with yellow-white fangs and claws. They were very large and they were approaching the hotel at an alarming speed. She rubbed her eyes. If there was someone out there in the water she certainly couldn't see them. It was hard to believe a person could survive in waves that size. Maybe something really is wrong with me, she thought; maybe I really *am* being borne away bit by bit. Maybe I'm going to get so small I'm going to have to live inside a drum like a fairy.

Penny directed her gaze across Marjorie's shoulder. "What on earth took you so long?" she asked. "Didn't you hear the timer go off?" She rose from her chair and began to walk swiftly toward the blue door on the far side of the room that led to the lobby. She was very light on her feet, Marjorie realized, much more graceful in motion than she'd looked sitting down. "Where were you?" Penny said to a girl who was just entering the dining room. "It was my job to watch *her,*" she said, pointing at Marjorie. "It was *your* job to watch the pie."

The girl appeared to be a little younger than Penny but she was nowhere near as tall and her eyes were an intense bright blue, the kind of color not usually associated with transparent things but with things made of metal like weapons or tools, things that reflected external light but never generated it from within. Aside from her eyes, though, the new girl was a perfect replica of sixteen-year-old Mary—so exact that Marjorie practically fainted at the sight of her. What if Mary was dead and she was seeing Mary's ghost? She didn't rule out the possibility based on the new girl's eyes, since everyone knew that eye color was one of the first things to undergo change in the afterlife.

The two girls embraced vigorously, kissing on the lips and sending their white arms and fingers all around and over one another. Then they came and joined Marjorie at the table.

Blue-Eyes was dressed in the same school uniform as Penny: a blue pleated skirt, a white blouse with a Peter Pan collar buttoned all the way to the top, a blue vest embroidered with the school emblem of a flaming child superimposed on a snowflake the same size as the child. On Penny the uniform had a crisp, fresh look; on Blue-Eyes it looked rumpled and damp, not unlike her hair, but maybe that was due to the fact that her hair was as limp and in need of washing as her mother's often used to be. The girl's skin, though, emitted waves of coolness the way a person's skin does after swimming, and there was a blue tint to her lips, which were chapped and ragged as if she'd been chewing on them.

By now the sea had calmed down, the sky resting its palm soothingly across the face of the water. The first scow Marjorie had seen since leaving home appeared, moving very slowly and up so high she could barely tell what it was. Like a gleaming grain of rice, she thought—whereas no matter how far above the sea the scow's operator managed to get, the sea would never look small to him.

"I've heard my mother talk about you," Blue-Eyes said to her. "The two of you used to be friends—that's what my mother told me. She used to live next door to you."

"That's where I still live," Marjorie said. "I haven't gone anywhere. Your mother's the one who moved away."

She tried to remember the last time she'd actually been inside number 49. At what point did the community association decide a person wasn't coming back? They would send her dog to the pound and if no one found him as sweet as she did, he'd be put to sleep. Then there would be an estate sale and complete strangers would walk around inside her house, handling her private things, all of which would have price tags on them.

She couldn't remember ever having said who she was, either, but both girls seemed to know.

"What do you mean you haven't gone anywhere?" Penny asked. "You're *here*, aren't you?"

Blue-Eyes took Marjorie's hand. "Do you ever see her?" she asked. "Did you see my mother before coming here?" She leaned forward and stared at her intently. "She was a nice girl, wasn't she? Did she give you a present for me?"

Marjorie tried to remember. As a girl, Mary had never been what you'd call "nice." The fact is, she could be moody and difficult to get along with. The other question was easier to answer, since Mary had never given her anything, but Blue-Eyes didn't let her have the chance.

"Was she a good student?" she asked.

"She was a very hard worker." Marjorie felt herself being wrung out like a piece of laundry. "She was the class artist."

"I *know* that." Blue-Eyes moved closer, bringing with her

the chill of her skin, which felt very different from the deep interior chill of Marjorie's own body. "What about my father? You knew him too, didn't you?"

Out of all the memories left to her, Marjorie realized, and they were few and far between, she seemed to have held onto this one. It was like a dream, only it had happened. She and the sorcerer were sitting in a booth at the Captain's Table, the waiter about to arrive to take their order. She was wearing a black dress of the heavy lustrous fabric they stopped making years ago and it set off her skin—back then she allowed just the right amount of animal fat in her diet to keep it creamy, and she hydrated enough to keep it translucent. "Do you always have to be such a goody-goody, Vicky dear?" the sorcerer was saying, lighting a cigarette for her even though he knew she didn't smoke. "Keep the boy busy," he instructed, and when she said "What boy?" he looked at her like she was one of the special children in room 12. Then he jumped up and took off down the hall after Mary. It was prom night; she had been a chaperone, though you couldn't exactly say she'd done such a great job of it.

"Yes," Marjorie said. "I knew your father. But it was a very long time ago."

When the sorcerer returned, she remembered, he never took his eyes off her. What he was doing was keeping a firm grip on her gaze so she wouldn't notice what he was really up to.

"The only human being he's ever cared about is your mother," Marjorie said.

"He cares about *me*," Blue-Eyes said. "Of course that's different."

A bell sounded, once, a single loud *ding*. "The timer!" Blue-Eyes said, jumping up and disappearing into the kitchen.

Once she was gone, Penny leaned closer, blinking her eyes at Miss Vicks and looking out at her from under her lashes.

"When she gets this way you have to ignore her," she said. "She's not like you and me."

That was exactly what the sorcerer said, Marjorie thought, a million years ago.

None of it mattered anymore. There hadn't been so many cars back then but even so everyone had to be careful—the kind of vigilance Marjorie had felt called upon to exercise ceaselessly seemed nowhere in evidence now. The sorcerer's silver-gray car appeared out of nowhere; Mary's forehead was spangled with stars. Eddie's parents collected money to have a memorial put up. But the past was over. It was gone. It wasn't *anything*.

When Blue-Eyes returned from the kitchen she was bearing a cherry pie between two pot holders. "Look what I found," she said, waving the pie under Marjorie's nose.

It smelled wonderful; as Blue-Eyes began to slice into it Marjorie could see the cherries bursting with juice. She tried to remember the last time she'd eaten anything—it had to have been before she rode off on the horse. She had been sitting on her living room sofa with a tray table in front of her, eating macaroni and cheese and watching the console. A man wearing what looked like a hazmat suit was balancing what looked like a pie on a broomstick, trying to get from point A to point B without dropping the pie while an enormous clock like the one in her classroom at school kept ticking. It was a funnier pie than the one Blue-Eyes had just brought in from the kitchen—something like banana custard, the kind of pie designed to make the man look especially stupid when he dropped it on his head. But before that happened she'd heard the thump and ran to the window.

"What do you think you're doing?" Penny whirled to face Blue-Eyes. "The pie got burned! Don't you ever listen? Sometimes a pie is really burned and you have to throw it in the garbage. Sometimes a person really dies."

"I have no idea what you're talking about," Blue-Eyes said. She removed a slice carefully and set it on one of the waiting dessert plates. "Guests first," she said, handing the plate to Marjorie.

"No!" Penny said. "You can't make her eat that!" She turned to her and Marjorie could see that she was starting to cry. "You're a teacher," Penny said. "You know the story of the girl who ate the seeds—I think she's the one I mean. Maybe I'm thinking of the hunters who lost their way. I used to know which story was which."

"For heaven's sake," Blue-Eyes said. "Why don't you just calm down?" She folded her hands in what looked to Marjorie like a parody of piety.

By now the sun had come all the way out and was shining brightly, setting sparks flying everywhere across the dancing waves. *Brigadoon,* Miss Vicks thought. Before the photographer appeared with his horse—before she got up on the horse and rode away—she had been listening to a group of girls singing as they walked along the street. "There may be other days as rich and rare," she remembered the girls singing, "there may be other springs as full and fair. But they won't be the same—they'll come and go . . ."

"Please oh please!" Penny said. "Don't eat it! I beg of you!"

The dining room was warm and she had thawed out completely. Marjorie Vicks, Miss Vicks, Vicks, M., Vicky Dear—whoever on earth she was she had never felt so hungry in her life, and despite her own worst fears she hadn't melted away. When she picked up her fork, to her delight she saw that her hand looked the way it used to when she wasn't much older than Penny and Blue-Eyes, the ropy veins and the brown spots gone, and in their place the creamy, hydrated skin of her youth.

Things couldn't be more perfect, Marjorie thought, three girls sitting together in the sunshine, their lives ahead of them. By now the water had come so close to the hotel that if a window were to be opened she could reach out and her hand would get wet. The water was bright blue like the girls' uniforms, the shade of blue in a regular-sized box of crayons. Luckily the windows weren't open, though, because if they were, the water would be coming into the dining room and everything would end up soaked.

She could hear the same rattling noise she'd heard the night before that sounded like it was made by a dog collar. It seemed to be coming from the other side of the blue door leading to the hotel lobby. She took her first bite of pie. "If only I'd known they allowed dogs," she said, "I'd have brought mine."

"That *is* your dog," Penny said. "You know that, don't you?"

"My dog?" Marjorie started to get up but Blue-Eyes pushed her back down into her chair. "I thought by now he'd have been taken away to the pound," she said. "I thought he was dead."

Blue-Eyes started to laugh. "Just where do you think you are, anyway?" she said.

It was then that Marjorie looked up from her plate and saw the infernal thing. It was sitting across the table from her, hunched over and chewing with its mouth open, cherries spilling out of its mouth and onto the tablecloth. It looked just like Blue-Eyes—probably even its own mother couldn't tell them apart.

Descent of the Aquanauts

EVERYBODY THINKS IT'S GOING TO BE DIFFERENT FOR them, Janice said. The dinosaurs thought so too. She was on the porch of her rental duplex, busy smearing her thighs with suntan lotion, her tan an enviable deep golden-brown. By this time Janice had been at the shore for a month. Golden-brown was the color everyone craved, not only for their body parts but for their food.

The dinosaurs had small brains, one of the girls said. All of us were older now; we'd learned things in school. Everyone thought the sun went around the earth, then everyone thought the earth went around the sun. Who knew what they'd be thinking next? The moon came out of the place where the ocean is now. The moon came from outer space and the earth captured it in its orbit.

The moon, Janice said. The moon was what started all the trouble. She finished her thighs and started in on her arms. She took her time, squeezing the lotion out bit by bit and rubbing it into her skin in small circular motions; she was driving the little girls crazy. They'd promised their mothers they wouldn't go to the beach without her. You couldn't apply lotion on the beach—that was Janice's rule. If you waited until you got to the beach, sand would get in the lotion, spoiling your tan.

Janice informed everyone that after her husband arrived Friday they were taking a moonlit cruise on a luxury sailboat. She hadn't married the boyfriend with the two-tone car; he turned out to be unreliable, meaning he dumped her for someone better looking. The man she married was named Henry and everyone thought he was too nice for Janice. He had the appearance of an English gentleman, very delicate and pale, the way a hermit crab looks between shells. Henry treated everyone with kindness. One of the little girls said he asked to see her peehole, but it was common knowledge he liked Janice best.

After two people got married everything that had formerly seemed interesting became uninteresting—this was common knowledge too. Once you were married, romance and heartbreak were no longer an option. Where were the surprises? When she wasn't wearing a bathing suit, Janice wore a girdle under her clothes. She didn't have a pussy anymore, she had genitals. Her nipples disappeared in one big thing called a bosom.

You girls know nothing, Janice said, lighting a cigarette and blowing smoke rings. The sky was the usual color, a solid shade of blue that suggested everything worth seeing lay behind it. This was also true of the houses on either side of the street, two rows of identical white duplexes, like the semi-detached brick houses back home. The only way you could tell the duplexes apart was by their awnings—Janice's was forest green with yellow stripes.

The curly-haired girl came walking down the stairs from the second floor with her raft under her arm. Have any of you ever *looked* at the moon? she asked. The raft was the same color green as the green of Janice's awning, the canvas so old and dry that until the girl got it into the water it made her skin creep. If you look at the moon you see it's something different from what they teach you, the girl said. She'd been

planning to go to the beach alone but when she overheard
Janice talking about the moon she couldn't resist joining
in. Stars around the silver moon hide their silverness when
she shines upon the earth, the girl said, quoting her favorite
poet. Upon the black earth.

It used to be too dangerous to go on moonlit cruises,
Janice continued. Once she got started she was unstoppable.
The thing about the moon is how it makes things happen
just by being there, like the way it can pull all the water on
one side of the planet into a big bulge and then let it go.
That's why there are tides.

I wish I could go on a cruise, someone said.

My dad says those cruises are highway robbery, said someone else.

It was a block and a half from the duplex to the boardwalk. The sidewalk was so hot the curly-haired girl could feel
it through the soles of her flip-flops. The grass was yellow,
the hydrangeas blue. The ocean was a wobbly sliver of light
even brighter than the sky and shimmering like a mirage—
she could hardly wait to get there.

The cruise is worth it, Janice corrected. Ab-so-tive-ly
pos-i-lute-ly. She said it helped if you were a newlywed. She
leaned forward to put out her cigarette on the sidewalk,
and when she sat up everyone held their breath to see if her
bosom was going to stay inside her suit. The thing I'm talking about happened long ago, Janice said. Not as long ago as
the Rain of Beads but a thousand times worse. People used
to think the Horsewomen were involved, only this was another group. They were older and they were human girls and
they had a leader—they called themselves the Aquanauts.
Their leader was a girl who no longer cared what anyone
thought about her. She no longer cared if everyone thought
she was weird. During the week there were only women and
children at the shore, just like now. The men came on the

weekends. If the men had been there probably none of this would have happened.

People went to the shore then? someone asked.

You think vacation is something new? Janice laughed the laugh she'd been working on, one that was supposed to sound musical.

If the men were there it wouldn't have made any difference, someone said. I've heard about the Aquanauts. What happened had nothing to do with what sex people were.

Across the street the mother of one of the little girls had appeared in her driveway in a red bikini, a lit cigarette gripped between her lips as she hosed down her convertible. The mothers didn't pay Janice for keeping an eye on their daughters, but they made it worthwhile for her, occasionally inviting her and her husband to their parties. Otherwise Janice wouldn't have had any social life to speak of, she knew that, just as she knew the reason why had something to do with her being unsuitable in some way she couldn't put her finger on, but that she suspected had to do with the fact that she, unlike the mothers, spent so much time with their daughters. It would be different when she had a daughter of her own.

In the beginning the group was like Pangaea, Janice said—that was how they got their power. They were like one giant lump of land surrounded by a single giant sea. It wasn't until the lump broke into pieces that you could tell from the fossils how it used to be. One girl had a black locket that used to belong to another girl's mother, one girl had another girl's friendship ring. One girl had another girl's handknitted argyle socks. One girl stole. She stole Blue Boy from Pinkie in the pack of trading cards in another girl's cigar box, breaking up that treasured pair forever. Of course the girls didn't like each other equally. When they played Nancy

Drew someone always got left out, frequently the girl who stole, who refused to be Bess, while the girl who didn't care what anyone thought of her was always George. She came from very far away and then one day she disappeared. In between she lived on the second floor of a duplex apartment at the shore.

When I say *girls*, Janice said, I mean *teenagers*.

How many girls were there? someone asked. By now everyone knew better than to ask their names.

What difference does it make? I don't know, Janice said. Maybe four. Maybe five. Not a big group.

I have a black locket, someone said.

Do you think I'm blind? said Janice. And don't everyone go telling me about your friendship rings.

A hot breeze gusted off the bay, riddled with flies. Janice swatted at them but they kept landing on her; they were attracted to the suntan lotion. If she knew who'd taken Blue Boy she wasn't saying.

The Aquanauts always waited until the families had left the beach and gone home, Janice said. It added to the girls' feeling of power to think of what was going on in the duplexes without them there. Everyone's bathing suit had a crotch full of heavy gray sand and you had to be careful not to make a mess in the bathroom when you peeled it off. On weekends the fathers mixed cocktails and opened cherrystones while the mothers mixed cocktail sauce. During the week the mothers did it all themselves. If you were a good girl you sat on the duplex porch with your mother while she painted your fingernails bright red to match hers. She drank a martini and you drank apricot nectar. The little sisters played with their Ginny dolls, the Ginnies who couldn't walk and the Ginnies who could, though you wouldn't really call what they did "walking."

By the time the girls got to the beach the sun was on its way into the bay on the other side of the island, and the shadows of the boardwalk shops and amusement park rides had grown longer and longer, making the sand dark and cool. The two lifeguards had turned over their chair and their lifeboat and taken off their whistles, dreaming of kissing the same girls they'd spent the whole day protecting. The beach was empty except for the gulls and the things people left behind accidentally like wristwatches and shoes or on purpose like trash. The sand castles had been swallowed by the sea. It was low tide, the shadow of the top car of the Ferris wheel swinging back and forth at the edge of the water.

I like the black-haired lifeguard, said one of the older girls.

He likes you, too, said another girl. I can tell.

What about the man with the metal detector? said the curly-haired girl's little sister. The man with the metal detector was always one of the last people to leave the beach. Her heart went out to him, with his overtall red crew cut and the way the sleeves of his white short-sleeved shirt stuck out like fairy wings.

Don't be stupid, said someone else. This happened before any of us were born.

What difference does it make? said the curly-haired girl. It could have happened yesterday.

Every night it was the same thing, Janice said. The girls would wait until the beach was dark and then they would walk straight into the ocean and swim away from shore until they disappeared. Afterward they would sit under the boardwalk and get so drunk that by the time they came home and went to bed it seemed to all of them that they were like clothes tumbling around in a dryer.

One night something different happened. The girls didn't come back. The mothers were sitting on the duplex porches, smoking cigarettes and drinking cocktails. They were sitting in groups of two or three, the fathers still in the city. Some of the fathers also were sitting on their porches at home, drinking and smoking and listening to the hot summer wind moving through the crowns of the sycamore trees. The fathers weren't in groups; aside from the ones having affairs they were alone. There was a feeling of melancholy everywhere, the melancholy of being in a place apart from the person with whom you normally spent your time, thinking of her sipping her martini, picturing the lit tip of his cigarette traveling in darkness away from his lips and toward the ashtray. The sound in the other person's ears of a car turning onto the street where the two of you normally lived. The sound of the sea in your own ears. The feeling of melancholy was everywhere and it wasn't, generally, such a terrible feeling. Because everyone knew they were going to be reunited with the person they were missing, they could throw themselves into their melancholy mood.

There had been warnings. But people never heed warnings.

No one listened, and as more and more people stopped listening, more and more people stopped telling the truth. Even Madame X didn't tell the truth, having been designed that way by the chamber of commerce. Nothing will put a bigger damper on a family vacation than being told the world's about to end.

You've seen how she just sits there in her glass case in the arcade, Janice said, with her big glass eyes and her little plaster hands lifted like the pope's, waiting for the next coin to drop. That night she decided—no more lies. Supposedly it was one of the lifeguards who got the fortune, but he didn't take it seriously. The only thing lifeguards take seriously is looking good for girls. You don't belong here, the fortune said. You never have. Once the land stops getting in its way, the ocean is going to be everywhere.

Madame X told me I was lucky in matters pertaining to business and finance, someone said.

She told me I was going to meet a dark, handsome stranger, said someone else.

I bet she meant the lifeguard, said one of the little sisters.

Girls, Janice said, oh girls. For a moment she stared off into space like she was trying to collect herself. The parents didn't realize anything was different, she said, and she sounded angry. Not at first. If they'd been paying attention to the moon they might have had a clue, but they were too filled with feelings of nostalgia and self-pity, the way adults become after they've been drinking. The girls knew it was going to happen that night though and they were ready. Their leader said she hoped they'd said their good-byes. Everyone had brought her air hose, for all the good it would do.

It was late and the tide was as low as it gets. The girls didn't think they'd ever had to walk so far before arriving at the water. They walked and walked and walked and meanwhile the moon was practically on top of them, like they could touch it. Like they could stick a finger in one of the craters—you've all seen the moon do that.

My dad says that's just an optical illusion, someone said.

If your dad's such a genius why did he ever have you? said someone else.

The curly-haired girl moved a little closer. I wouldn't dream of touching the moon with my two arms, she said. She was quoting the poet again but no one cared. They were too busy listening to Janice. Even the curly-haired girl couldn't leave. That was the thing about Janice—she made you want to know where she was taking you, even if you didn't want to go.

After what seemed like forever the girls got to the water, Janice continued. There had been a sea breeze all day long. Now there was nothing except a feeling like something holding its breath. The girls waded in, enjoying the warm water on their feet and the burst of the first waves against their ankles, still warm but cooler, the shallow water mixing with water from the heart of the ocean, which was cold. The ocean is coldhearted, you don't have to be a genius to know that. It makes boats sink. It makes you watch where you put your feet. If you choose to swim at the end of the day after the lifeguards have left the beach you take your life in your hands. You know that, don't you? Janice gave everyone a piercing stare meant to drive her point home.

As usual the girls were dressed in identical black bathing suits with skirts and identical white rubber bathing caps that strapped under the chin. They looked like old ladies. They didn't enter the water like old ladies, though, splashing water up over the tender parts of themselves to lessen the shock. The girls plunged right in and kept on going. They ignored the jellyfish and the seaweed. They didn't look back. At their leader's command they dove under the first big breaker that came their way and rose up on the other side at the exact same time as meanwhile the whole idea of what a wave is fell apart behind them. For a moment they paused so everyone except the girl who was so nearsighted she couldn't see anything without her glasses had a chance to make eye contact with one another. Then they kept on swimming.

The girls had been preparing for this for a long time. At the shore they practiced in the ocean; at home they practiced in the bathtub. At first they just held their breath, but after a while they got so they could breathe underwater. The girls didn't really need the hoses anymore; they just brought them along for backup. People were eighty percent water, they figured. What made everyone think the moment our ancestors came out of the water and started to breathe air represented a step up the evolutionary ladder? Why did people always think things got better by moving forward? Why did people think that way? It was so limited! As if the surface was somehow better than everything else. As if *air* was king.

The girls rose on the next wave and felt themselves flung forward as the wave broke behind them. The farther they got from shore the bigger the waves were becoming, rocking under them with more and more energy. It was like they were being pushed on a swing, higher and higher, getting swept up the side of a hill to stay for a split second at the top before being swept down into the valley below and then up again, the top even higher this time, the slope even steeper and the valley lower, until they found themselves at the top of a mountain of water the size of an alp. The moon was right there above them, drawing the ocean up to it. The girls practically banged their heads against its surface. Because of the moonlight everything looked like it was coated in silver, but you could see how dark the water was underneath the coating, so dark green it was almost black, and the moon itself was whiter than anything, whiter and smoother than an egg.

I've had that dream, someone said. I dream about those kinds of waves a lot.

It's an ancestral memory, Janice explained primly, as if she was mentioning something better left unsaid.

The girls didn't realize until they'd arrived at the top of that final wave that one of their group was missing. You'd probably guess it was the girl with the bad eyesight, but you'd be wrong. The girl with the bad eyesight was right there treading water with the rest of them, waiting for the signal from the leader to dive under. No, it was another girl, one of the best swimmers. Unfortunately for her, or maybe fortunately—who can say?—she didn't always concentrate on what she was doing. She was careless, and when people are careless things go wrong.

Somewhere along the line, Janice said, the careless girl let herself get caught in a breaker that carried her back to the beach. The breaker curved over her head and thumped her from behind—that's the kind of thing that happens when you're thinking about something else, like for instance a boy. Then it churned her around and around before leaving her on her stomach in the sand together with a lot of broken clamshells and those little crabs the size of your thumbnail. Even though nobody was there to see her, the girl stopped to make sure her bathing suit was still in place before getting to her feet. Normally she didn't care about the way she looked, but this was different. The world was about to end and her friends had left her behind. They were going to survive and she was doomed. Plus she had to go home to her parents.

Except it didn't end, someone said. How can we be here if the world already ended?

I'm getting hot, said someone else. When do we get to go to the beach?

A lot of people died, Janice said. You've studied it in school. The world didn't actually come to an end, but it might as well have. It was like scientists predicted. Whole countries weren't there anymore. You've all seen the globe. It looked completely different.

Suddenly she yawned and stretched and stood up. Well, come on, she said. What are you waiting for?

The beach was just a block and a half away but it always took longer to get there than it should. The little girls had to be herded along and there were lots of things to carry. Things got dropped and someone had to go back to pick them up. By the time they arrived at their usual spot—a good spot just to the left of the lifeguard stand with no one between them and the water—the sun was directly overhead. Janice screwed the umbrella into the sand while the older girls spread their towels as far from the umbrella and as close to the lifeguard as they could get. The beach was crowded. Everyone was talking at the top of their lungs about private matters like heartbreak and terminal illness. It was the only way to be heard over the sound of everyone else, not to mention the surf.

Hurry up! Hurry up! cried the little girls.

It's not like the ocean is *going* anywhere, Janice pointed out.

A seaplane flew past very low over the water, trailing a banner that said "Take a Moonlight Cruise on the Evening Star."

Come Friday, Janice said, that's going to be me and my honey on that boat. She set up her beach chair in the pool of shade made by the umbrella and sank into it, letting out a sigh.

It was a very young coast. The little girls went off to play with their buckets and shovels in the shallows while the older girls began working on their tans. One minute there was no wind at all, the next minute it came gusting off the bay. Some sheets of newspaper drifted past, followed by a baby wearing nothing. The lifeguards whistled in a swimmer who'd ventured too far out.

People are such idiots, Janice said. She reached into her beach bag and withdrew her cigarettes and her sunglasses. You know they're still down there, she said, lowering her voice. The Aquanauts are still down there. They live in the deepest part of the ocean where it's so dark you can't see what they look like. They don't look the way they did before the Descent. They used to care how they looked. They used to shave their legs, for instance, things like that.

The curly-haired girl knew Janice was talking about her. She thought it was probably a good idea to like being looked at if you were a girl—it was probably key to survival. If you were a gorilla it was the other way around. Somewhere the girl had read that if you looked a gorilla in the eye it would strangle you.

Whatever we can't see has power over us, Janice said.

Plus, as much as people seem to think so, the ocean isn't infinite.

When that immense wave broke it went everywhere. Almost everywhere, Janice corrected herself—emphasizing *almost*—but not quite. You can't even begin to imagine what it looked like. Luckily it was nighttime. If it had happened during the day it would have been even more terrifying. The whole sky was blocked out. Some people ran, some people got in their cars. They ran the way people do in horror movies, looking back over their shoulder while continuing to run forward, without any sense of direction or purpose. Of course it did no good. The only things with a chance of making it were the things living in the water. Even then, a lot of them didn't do so well.

But the Aquanauts were OK, right? someone said.

Look! said someone else, laughing. The tide was coming in and just as Janice was talking about the immense wave breaking, a small wave had broken and sent parts of itself up over the sand and onto the bottom edge of someone's beach towel. As the water crept up the beach it turned the white sand dark, pocking it with tiny holes where the sand crabs lived. Then it went back where it had come from. The air smelled like hot tar. The bucket-shaped things the little girls had been building got washed away along with other things like sheets of newspaper and flip-flops and cigarette butts.

Where do you think *you're* going? Janice asked the curly-haired girl.

The girl was heading out into the water with her raft under her arm.

Didn't you hear what I was just saying? Janice asked. About the Aquanauts?

So? said the girl. Vacation was a nightmare when you were a teenage girl forced to live in a rented duplex so small and with such thin walls that the sounds and smells of your whole family not to mention the people downstairs like Janice and her husband were always *right there*. The curly-haired girl knew Janice and her husband could hear her feet walking across their ceiling. While they were having sexual intercourse they could hear her feet. Janice could hear her feet while Henry's penis went in and out of her.

Maybe you don't get it, Janice said. This is no joke. Because I've watched you—you're always one of the ones they have to whistle in.

At first the girls just spent their time playing, she explained. They couldn't believe how lucky they were. They were alive and they could go anywhere they wanted. They could explore the parts of the ocean where human beings had never been before, and they could swim through the top floors of skyscrapers and into places like maximum security prisons and movie stars' mansions and the lion cage at the zoo, places that had always been off-limits to ordinary people. It seemed like nothing could hurt them, either. Not even sharks or giant squids, and they didn't get sick with things like gill rot or white fin the way regular fish did.

But after a while it was like, what's the point? A lot of time went by. The water receded. The descendants of the people who hadn't died began reproducing. First they did it as a necessity. It was only later they started enjoying it. Soon things were back to the way they'd been before the wave. Houses got built, streets like this one with rows of duplexes. Someone put up a boardwalk. There was a penny arcade with a fortune-teller in a glass case. This was possible because it turned out the future still existed. It's the one we have now, in case you wondered.

A whole lot of time had gone by but the girls hadn't gotten any older. They were still girls. Even after everything that had happened to them, that part never changed. Eventually they found themselves back at their old beach. They recognized it from the shadow of the Ferris wheel down by the water.

Janice pointed and the little girls gasped.

Our beach? someone asked.

What did you expect? said someone else. That's how history works, or else Janice wouldn't know it.

The girls couldn't get out of the water to lie on the sand and work on their tans. If they got out of the water they couldn't breathe, and they missed the way the lifeguards used to look at them. They didn't want to stay girls forever. That's the main thing about girls, am I right? Janice held out her left arm and studied it critically, admiring her tan and the way her ring sparkled in the sun. Girls are always in a big hurry to take the next step, she said, the one about men and romance and marriage and babies. The girls drifted as close to shore as they could without being seen. They could hear the sound of baseball games on people's radios. The lifeguards were looking out to sea but the girls knew they weren't looking for *them*. Each girl was crying but the other girls couldn't tell because her face was already wet.

It's their own fault, someone said. They were the ones who decided to live undersea. No one made them do it.

If they hadn't they probably would have died, said someone else.

They'd be dead now anyway, said the curly-haired girl. She turned her back on the group and began walking toward the water.

After Janice finished moving the umbrella and all the beach things from the path of the incoming tide, she spread herself out on her towel, flat and wide and brown like a gingerbread man. Except they aren't, Janice said. The girls aren't dead and they aren't ever going to die. You'd think that was a good thing, wouldn't you? But what if you wanted to take the next step only you were doomed to be a teenage girl forever? It would make you angry, wouldn't it? It would make you more than angry. It would fill you with murderous rage.

The girls got to be immortal and it made them deadly.

At first there didn't seem to be anything to worry about. Sometimes people said they felt something swim by them in the ocean but that was all. Sometimes the girls would bump against someone but just barely—the girls called that "kissing." Of course they no longer wore their black bathing suits and their white rubber bathing caps—when a girl bumped into someone the person could feel how seamless the girl's skin was. Their skin felt smooth and slippery like sausage casings. It wasn't really skin, though. It was more like a pod.

After a while the girls began to shoot right past us, not quite seeing us and just barely feeling the bump of us against their skin. It was like all we were to them was something that got in their way. It was like they hated us.

I've felt that, someone said. I thought there was a fish swimming by me.

My mom said it was nothing to worry about, said someone else. It's only the current.

By now the curly-haired girl had gotten past the breakers and was lying on her stomach on her raft, paddling away from shore. She could see the moon up ahead, preparing to shine once the sun got out of its way. Every night there were more planets; planets were being born somewhere in space, calving off larger, older planets. This was the way of the universe, the old making way for the new. When she looked back the lifeguard stand was like a dollhouse toy, Janice like a dollhouse doll. Over the boardwalk the sky had turned the color of beets, but right above her head it was still blue and getting darker, the weird blue of a newborn baby's eyes.

It was then that the girl sensed it—a disturbance in the water next to the raft, a feeling of a presence getting ready to move past her and then pausing, sensing her there as well. She could see a glimmer of skin just below the surface, a shudder in the current as the head came up beside her. Whatever it was smelled like fish but also like it had been buried in dirt and was starting to decompose.

She could see where the stories came from. The thing's eyes were large and lustrous as plums, and when they stared at the girl they were filled with an intention so forceful she knew she couldn't be imagining it. Until that moment neither one of them had any idea of the other's existence, like the way a baby is suddenly in the world, or a dead person out of it. The thing's gaze was fixed on a place right above the girl's head, the place where she knew her thoughts were visible.

Back on shore no one noticed anything. People were eating hot dogs and burying one another in the sand. They opened her up and there it was, someone was saying in a loud voice. A tumor the size of a grapefruit.

Janice rolled over. You're probably wondering how those girls got to be that way, she said. Because they started out the same as you and me, just like everyone else.

They were all somebody's darlings, Janice said. They got tucked in, they got presents. They got Suzuki-method piano lessons. Also My Little Pony and Felicity the American Girl, horseback-riding lessons, religious training, ballet lessons, and pets. Also bedtime stories when the nights grew dark. Once upon a time there was a little girl who could be anything she wanted.

Later she couldn't remember she'd ever even had a mother or a father.

My mom and dad had *me*, said one of the little girls.

But what about that other girl? someone asked. The careless girl who got caught in the breaker?

She's the one who had to watch it happen, Janice said. She saw everything. The bad news is you're all descended from

her. That's why you have trouble sleeping—and don't go trying to tell me you don't because I know what goes on here at
night. The bedroom walls are like paper. The good news is
it'll start getting better once you're older. Cocktails at five—
that's the answer. If those mothers and fathers hadn't been
drinking their cocktails when the wave broke—if they'd been
able to see what was going on, the way the first spray was
very light, almost unnoticeable, but that it was followed by a
disturbance in the air that was everywhere and was a threat
to the whole idea of air, to the idea of breathing air instead
of water—if those mothers and fathers hadn't been drinking
cocktails then we'd have gone insane long ago.

In our house my dad's the one who drinks, someone said.

My mom drinks soda, said someone else. But my granny
drinks rubbing alcohol.

Suddenly the dark-haired lifeguard stood on the seat of
his stand and began blowing his whistle over and over again,
louder and louder, violently waving his arms, motioning toward shore.

Speaking of cocktails, Janice said. She looked at the sky
and then she looked at her wrist. The sun is over the yardarm,
she said; no one knew what she was talking about. She began
gathering together the things they'd brought with them to
the beach. They were all beginning to gather their things
together—it was as if a signal had gone off somewhere.

We can't leave now, said the curly-haired girl's little sister.
Even though she was often embarrassed by her older sister,
she didn't want her to die. She remembered the time she
dreamed her older sister died and it was terrible. She couldn't
stop thinking of Cinderella singing "a dream is a wish your
heart makes."

Both lifeguards had jumped down from their stand and
were dragging their boat across the sand and into the water.

Janice seemed affronted. The problem with humans is they

think their children are *theirs,* she said. They think because their children came from their own bodies and cells they *own* them, like where we come from points to the future.

By now most of the people leaving the beach had stopped in their tracks and were turned to face the water. The lifeboat rose and fell as the dark-haired lifeguard rowed it through the breakers, the oars lifting and lowering like wings on either side.

Does anyone know who it is? someone asked.

The stuck-up girl, someone said.

It's that poetry girl, said someone else.

Of course the girl couldn't hear them, she was so far out to sea on her raft. My darling, my dearest, she said. She had no way of knowing who she was talking to. How long had she been out there?

The sand at the water's edge was cold and hard, the galaxies revolving on their horizontal plane like a roulette wheel. From the shore all anyone could see was the lifeboat, getting smaller and smaller.

Believe me, you don't want to be here when they bring her back in, Janice said. It's not like I didn't tell her. You have to watch out for your arms and legs if you go that far out. You all heard me, right? The last girl this happened to had bites out of her.

Through the Wormhole

THE DAYS CAME AND WENT AND MARY KEPT GETTING older. It had been bound to happen. Her ears worked less effectively, one of them devising a high-pitched noise all its own. The noise reminded her of summer nights and the fathers appearing on the porches, each one with a different way of letting you know it was time for bed. Eddie's father would put two fingers in his mouth and whistle; Mr. Andersen used a conch shell. It would get dark, the street lamps would be lit, the girls would be singing a sad song as they gathered their trading cards together and said goodnight to one another. Romance was in the air, romance and false hope, not exactly the same thing but linked, like love and marriage. It was all the girls could think of.

My ear is driving me crazy, Mary told Walter as they lay together in bed. She knew better by now than to ask him if he heard what she was hearing. She would draw the curtains and he would open them, his shadow draping over her as he turned away from the window. They were in the vacation house he'd bought as a surprise for Mary—there was nothing intervening between it and the ocean. He thought the house would please her since she had fond memories of it from when she was a girl. Mary's hair had turned to dross, her skin to paper, but even so Walter liked looking at her.

What was happening to her was part of his original bargain, including the sorry condition of her teeth and eyes. The sight of Mary still had the power to arouse his desire. Then she would succumb to desire too, panting a little.

While her husband was at work in the city Mary sat staring at the ocean through the large half-moon-shaped front window. In the morning the waves were quite large but as the day wore on they grew smaller, almost too small to break, as if some long snakelike creature was tunneling along just below the surface. The days wore on, all of them; Mary rarely ventured forth into the sun until it had almost set. Sometimes St. Foy girls would march along the strand two by two in their blue uniforms. Sometimes they would run single file in their bare feet at the water's edge.

After graduation Blue-Eyes moved back to the city. Mary knew because Walter liked to fill her in on their daughter's exploits. For some time now she had been working with him; as far as Mary could tell she was doing very well. Occasionally there would be a story on the console involving Blue-Eyes. An interviewer would be asking her about Walter's latest project, the two of them standing together in an undisclosed location. Once Mary thought she recognized the koi pool in the park at the end of the street where she grew up. Blue-Eyes was talking about modern marriage, a subject Mary was sure her daughter knew nothing about. Blue-Eyes was explaining that she and the interviewer were standing not far from where her mother and father had met. "My father always said it was love at first sight," Blue-Eyes was saying. "What about your mother?" the interviewer wanted to know. "Oh, my mother." Blue-Eyes stared straight into the camera as if she knew Mary was watching. "You should ask her." She went on to say that whatever brought two people together had nothing to do with sex. It had to do with the abyss, the face of the deep, with whatever came before people or animals or life of any kind and what would be left after they were gone.

The way Blue-Eyes was dressed and wore her hair reminded Mary of the caryatids holding the porch roof of the Erechtheion atop their heads as they stared blankly at the wine-dark sea. The caryatids kept on staring even as pieces of their bodies broke off and fell into the water. According to gaze theory, what a person was looking at influenced how another person interpreted the first person's expression. It always surprised Mary how much she remembered from her art school days. From the quality of Blue-Eyes's gaze Mary could tell her daughter was looking at infinite space. She was looking at it and figuring out how she was going to be able to make it do her bidding.

"You should be pleased," Walter said, when Mary told him about the interview. "She got that from you."

"What do you mean from me?" Mary was at the sewing machine, turning out curtains.

He pointed. "The way you do that," he said. "She would hang on to your leg and watch your every move—I remember she seemed especially interested when you bit off a thread."

Mary considered. She didn't remember Blue-Eyes watching her do anything. It was true, she thought, that during Blue-Eyes's last year at St. Foy she had contacted Mary to ask her some question about measuring a bolt of a thing the name of which Mary couldn't quite hear because there was a lot of noise in the background that sounded like sewing machines but could just as well have been a bad connection or something so far beyond Mary's ability to know what it was it didn't even bear thinking about. They taught sewing at St. Foy, she knew that much, but when Mary asked Blue-Eyes if she would like a sewing basket of her own fitted with compartments for spools of thread and a pincushion and a measuring tape, Blue-Eyes informed her she was going to close the port. "A *sewing* basket, mother?" Blue-Eyes said. "You've never even tried to understand me."

Mary knew this wasn't true. In a way it was all she had done. The problem was, the bolt Blue-Eyes had unspooled from bore no relationship to Mary. They didn't make girls more ordinary than Mary had been. She was an ordinary person—that was the whole point.

When Mary was a girl and she went to the shore in the summer along with everyone else, she used to call the house she was living in now the chocolate-cheese house because the walls were pale yellow stucco, the trim dark brown. "It's called chocolate-cheese but you can't eat it!" she would announce whenever she and her parents walked past the house. The duplex her parents rented was in a different neighborhood altogether. The difference between a summer rental and a summer residence was like the difference between a human and a fairy. A famous actress had lived in Mary's house from 1930 to 1954, the same year the United States and Russia conducted aboveground atom bomb tests, releasing radioactivity into the atmosphere where it drifted for a while before settling into people's teeth and bones. Many things had been adrift then and always would be. The fishermen on a boat called *Lucky Dragon* had been especially unlucky, whereas the famous actress married a real live prince. A person could fill page after page with pieces of information like this—all you had to do was consult the console. Mary thought there was more information drifting through the world than there were stars in the sky. The famous actress's father had owned the business that supplied the bricks that the house Mary grew up in had been made out of and those bricks, like all bricks, kept leaking radioactivity. Not enough to do any harm, not even as much as the machine the shoe store used to X-ray her feet, but still. What good did it do to know this?

Accumulating a storehouse of information could do nothing to alter the fact that when she was a girl Mary had loved a boy and he had loved her. An exquisite bond had existed between them and something had broken that bond and now she would never see him again. He was gone.

"Dead and gone, dead and gone," tolled the bell buoys.

"What are you talking about?" asked the sewing machine, loyal, as ever, to Eddie.

"I could tell you his name but what difference would it make?" Mary replied, getting up out of her chair.

History with all its useless information kept unwinding behind her and in front of her like the movie Blue-Eyes had made out of chopsticks and shelf paper and a shoe box, a long scroll filled with information. It had been a seminal moment, Blue-Eyes told one of her interviewers.

Now Blue-Eyes lived with her partner, a word that reminded Mary of square dancing. The partner's name was Penny and it was obvious that she and Blue-Eyes felt sorry for Mary and Walter, imprisoned as they were in their modern marriage. The two women possessed a lot of information to corroborate their pity—everyone was so confident now, Mary thought. She supposed that was a good thing, especially if you were a girl.

She walked right up to the window. A shudder passed through the wet edge of the continent; the seabirds took off all at once from the jetty pilings. The problem with having information was that it made you feel like you ought to know when things were going to happen before they actually did. Mary put on her wide-brimmed straw hat and her sunglasses and her terry cover-up and headed for the beach. The beach was practically empty as it usually was at this hour, the young families having gone home to their summer rentals, leaving the prints of their feet behind in the soft white sand the water never reached except during a storm. Cindy

Duffy was waiting for Mary in one of the low-slung chairs she brought for them to sit in. She sat on the hard gray sand at the water's edge; every time a wave came in it got her butt wet.

"You're late," Cindy said to Mary.

"I was busy," Mary said.

Of course Cindy knew that she, Mary, was never busy, but she wasn't going to say so. Cindy, too, was wearing a wide-brimmed hat and sunglasses and a terry cover-up, the preferred beachwear for women of a certain age. It drove Mary crazy how Cindy made it look like she kept getting older when everyone knew she could go back to being pretty little Cindy XA at a moment's notice. She will never know sorrow, Mary thought, she will never know loss. Somehow these thoughts failed to console her. The act of pretending to get older had managed to confer a kind of dignity on the robot, making it hard to remember that in actuality it was the size and shape of a needle.

"Busy?" Cindy said. "Tell me about it." She released a *pouf* of exhaustion. "I've had the grandkids all week. Merrilee decided to stay in the city with Bill, and ever since Eddie got Roy that job with the Rockets I might as well be single."

Mary stared straight out to sea. The sea was a symbol of endlessness but of course it wasn't endless. Someone in a foreign land was staring back at her at this exact moment. Someone who spoke another language, someone who probably didn't wish her well but who was, finally, fathomable, not unlike the sea. "How many of them are there now?" she asked.

Cindy held up some fingers but Mary didn't turn her head to count. "It was nice of Eddie to help us out like that," Cindy said. "Roy's always felt he was born to be an announcer."

"He has the right voice for it," Mary said.

"I always thought Roy could have been an opera singer," Cindy said, and she sounded wistful.

It was a beautiful afternoon, the ocean ringed round with strings of clouds, the sky blue and clean. Cindy added more fingers. "Mary," she said. "Look at me. You know your time is almost up, right?"

"What do you mean?" Mary asked.

She understood perfectly, though. The fingers meant how much time she had left. The problem was she couldn't tell what unit of time Cindy was referring to. It could be years or months or weeks or days or hours or even—this was too terrible to consider—minutes. Whatever the unit was, she had six of them—three more than the number of Cindy and Roy's grandchildren she'd seen out of the corner of her eye.

The thing about a life is how hard it is to make it shift course once it's gotten going. There was no wind, no wind at all.

"It's up to you," Cindy said. "It's always been up to you. Eddie isn't going to be any help. He doesn't have the faintest idea what to do. He was just an immature form of the species when he got taken. A little boy, you'd say."

For some reason Mary found herself remembering a trip with the Darlings to a popular outlet store. Mary's mother had told her how much money she could spend on a sweater if she saw one she liked. The sweaters were more expensive than Mary thought they would be, the Darlings better off. The only sweater Mary could afford was a cardigan in an unpleasant shade of burnt orange, neither a style nor a color remotely in fashion—she knew when she bought it everyone would feel sorry for her. Driving home from the outlet store she shut the hem of her new sweater in the car door but she couldn't make herself tell Mrs. Darling what she'd done. The landscape swelled past, houses, trees, phone wires. My poor sweater, Mary thought. Enough of it had been left hanging out that it was probably dragging along the road.

Poor, poor sweater! She hated it for being so stupid; it had gotten what it deserved.

And now what? Mary thought.

"Now you have to give this all up," Cindy said. "*All* of it. Also you have to stop feeling sorry for yourself. The sweater no longer exists."

Mary had known the robot could read her mind but this was the first time it hadn't even bothered to pretend that it was doing something else.

"After you threw it away it was picked up by a scow," Cindy said. "Everything that went into its composition got broken down into parts too numerous and too infinitesimal to ever be brought together again into anything even re-motely resembling a sweater."

"Like the Rain of Beads?" Mary said.

"Oh, for heaven's sake! What is wrong with you people? The Rain of Beads? Get over it!" The robot's voice jumped to a register that made Mary's eyes water. For a moment she thought she could see something other than Cindy sit-ting in the chair beside her. "The Rain of Beads," the voice echoed, disgusted.

"If I leave him he isn't going to like it," Mary said.

"Of course he isn't going to like it."

Mary swallowed. It wasn't just that her eyes were water-ing, it was that she was crying. "What about Blue-Eyes?" she asked.

But the robot was done with her—she could feel it pierce her heart as it went.

Meanwhile the tide was coming in; Mary stood in the shallows where the littlest waves lapped around her ankles. The chairs were gone, the beach empty, it was growing dark. More than six minutes had passed, meaning the time she had left could be measured in hours, if not eons. Soon Walter would arrive home in his silver-gray car, the same car he'd taken Eddie away in. Then they would sit together watching the moon make a road of light on the water. His great melancholy golden eyes, his splendid nose with its curved nostrils like the drawer pulls on the highboy she inherited from her parents. If she left him it would be as good as admitting that practically her whole life had been a mistake.

She had just wrapped her cover-up tighter around the bag of bones that her body had turned out to be and begun to head back to the house when an even older woman caught her eye, trolling the dunes with a metal detector. She looked a little like Miss Vicks though of course it couldn't be her— Miss Vicks had been dead for years. Whether it was friend or foe, robot or fairy, it was impossible to say. There had been so many Miss Vickses, including the shy human woman.

"Hello, Dearie," the old woman said. "I don't suppose you have a spare piece of change lying around for a poor beggar woman like myself? I haven't had a thing to eat in days and this thing"—she lifted the metal detector and gave it a little shake—"is no use whatsoever."

"I don't have anything on me," Mary said. "But if you come up to the house, I'll see what I can do."

For a starving person, the old woman looked well fed, plump even; a bright spot of light, its source indiscernible, rode the surface of each eyeball, lending her a fervent, overstimulated look.

"I see you've done very well for yourself," the old woman said once they were inside. She was eyeing the curio cabinet where the sorcerer kept his collection of Mary-related flotsam, including the piece of blue-green beach glass he claimed was shaped like Mary's torso, the jar of small translucent shells he said were the color of her skin, and the glossy dark brown seedpod the size of a lady's compact he'd informed her was called a Mary bean. "No one wants to grow old," the old woman said. "No one wants to get left to grow moldy in a corner." She was still holding on to her metal detector, and when Mary offered to take it from her the old woman's eyes grew brighter still. "Have you made the sign of the cross, Dearie?" she asked. "Have you smoored the fire?"

There was no good answer to these questions. Mary went into the kitchen and opened the refrigerator. "I don't have much," she called. "How do you feel about leftovers?" During the week while Walter was away she didn't keep a lot of food in the house. She located some chicken à la king in a plastic tub near the back but it didn't look like it was good anymore.

The sound of merry-go-round music from the boardwalk drifted through the kitchen window—day had turned to night and Mary hadn't really noticed. Often she didn't. At low tide she would collect mussels, cook them in vermouth, and then drink whatever was left in the bottle. "How about some wine?" she asked, but there was no answer.

When Mary returned to the living room to see what had become of the old woman she found her opening the curio cabinet and reaching inside. "What do you think you're doing?" Mary asked. "Give me that!"

"Don't get all excited," the old woman said. "I only wanted to have a look." She cupped the Mary bean in the palm of her hand and stroked it like a pet, feeling around its edge with her finger. "Do you know how to open one of these?" she asked.

"No," Mary said. "I don't think that would be such a good idea." The bean came from a far-off land where it grew on a vine so huge a person could live inside it like a house. Some people considered it a charm against drowning, but according to Walter, the darker the color of the bean, the more dangerous its contents. They'll put anything in, he'd told her.

A car approached, its headlights riding the wall, lapping like water up and over the curio cabinet and toward the ceiling.

"That's *him*, isn't it?" The old woman handed Mary the bean and began sliding her metal detector back and forth across the floor at the foot of the wall. It made a series of whimpering noises punctuated with soft grunts, not unlike the sound a newborn puppy makes in its blind quest for its mother. "What are you waiting for?" the old woman scolded. "He'll be here any minute."

The car engine idled for a moment, then it cut off.

You couldn't get into one of those pods easily. Mary worked at prying it apart with a fingernail along the perimeter of what looked like some sort of seam.

"Hurry up!" said the old woman.

The lights outside brightened and went out; a car door slammed and as it did Mary felt a latch inside herself beginning to release. It was the smallest of latches but eventually she managed to force it open, not unlike the way she'd felt a million years ago letting out the baby. The chain of clouds strung around the ocean began to break into pieces. Everything was dividing into pieces to keep the parts clear. The heavens, the earth, the underworld—human beings have always needed divisions like that to know where they are and where they're going. "What are you doing?" the sorcerer cried, entering the house. The pod sprang open.

Mary Mary Mary she heard and she knew she'd heard that same voice before. The white wall in front of her had something that looked just like a door in it and the thing that looked like a door began to shake and disappear. There was no salt in the air behind it or sand on the floor like there was in her house. Carefully Mary made her way onto all fours and across what remained of the material world, but as far as she could tell there wasn't much of it left. She let her flesh down carefully, her face pointing straight ahead. I'm not ready to die yet, she was thinking.

Something pulled her through from the other side.

Downie

EDDIE WAS AN OLD MAN NOW. HIS HAIR WAS WHITE and his teeth false, the youthful promise of his career all but forgotten. The sorcerer had sold the Rockets to a company run by his daughter and the team was once again unbeatable, the company's business mysterious yet apparently dedicated to the pursuit of human immortality through the introduction of better materials into the finished product. He had also finally been persuaded to sell the family estate to the developer who built a long-awaited retirement community there, including the nursing home where Eddie's mother and father spent the last years of their lives. No one knew what the sorcerer planned to do with the fortune he made from these transactions; ever since his wife left him it was said that he spent most of his time brooding in the water tower.

As Eddie walked along the neat brick pathways of Woodard Village, he tried to picture the way the estate used to look—he seemed to remember a large ornamental pond where the buildings now stood. The day was mild, the air sweet but with a smell of autumn in it, of burning leaves, and in the blue sky he could see a small wavering V of geese making their way south, hear the plaintive far-off sound of their honking. Mary had always made fun of him, of the way the end of summer made him sad—her eyes would mock him, lovingly. He remembered how she would sit on her porch stoop with one of the other girls, the two of them apparently in deep negotiation for some card, a dog or a horse or what the girls all referred to as a "scene," meaning a painting from the Romantic era showing a world where beautiful places like the Woodard Estate had once existed. How innocent the girls' trades were, Eddie thought—he knew so little about it. Mary's head would be bent over the cigar box, her shoulders hunched, but he could tell she was more focused on him than she was on anything. No one or nothing else in his life had given him that same degree of attention.

Now an orderly approached on the path, pushing an old woman toward him in a wheelchair. The orderly was tall and heavyset and there was something about him that gave Eddie the feeling it was someone he knew. The old woman was just an old woman; she was wearing the kind of sunglasses with side shields a person needed after cataract surgery, and her long silver hair had been put up in a bun. "Where am I?" she kept asking the orderly; she seemed agitated. "What am I doing here?"

"Don't worry, gorgeous," the orderly replied. "You're right where you're supposed to be."

"Well, then," said the old woman. She seemed relieved, relaxing back into her chair only to lean forward once again at Eddie's approach. "Are you coming to lunch?" she asked. Her voice wavered slightly, the way a voice will after an arduous journey during which the speaker has turned from a woman to a beam of light and back again. "Today is Friday," she added, clapping together the swollen joints of her hands. "Swordfish!"

Eddie was about to say no, that while the place certainly seemed nice enough, he wasn't a resident. But then he was filled with a sense of terror. He felt cold; it suddenly came to him that not all that long ago he had been a young man, and that like his fellow human beings he'd always relied on meaninglessly small units for the measurement of time.

"Swordfish? Are you sure?" The orderly stopped dead in his tracks. "Swordfish mate for life," he pointed out, giving Eddie a look.

It was then that it came to him—this was Downie, his old friend from the ballpark. Not that they'd had all that much to do with one another. Eddie had been a star and Downie a mascot. But even so, Eddie had always felt like he and Downie had a special relationship, that Downie was keeping an extra-sharp eye on him, his vigilance having its basis in something that had nothing to do with baseball.

The three of them made their slow way along an avenue of shade trees, the leaves casting moving shadows across their faces. Eventually they found themselves in the large main building. "Whatever you do," the old woman told Downie, laughing, "don't push me down there." She was pointing toward the blue hallway that led to the level-three nursing home; when you entered that hallway you never came out again except as a cadaver.

"I wouldn't dream of it," said Downie. He gave Eddie another look before turning the wheelchair, and the next thing Eddie knew the old woman and Downie had suddenly disappeared around a bend, leaving him alone in the corridor.

Eddie was sure the people who ran Woodard Village did the best they could but there was no masking the smell that traveled up from the part of the building no one wanted to think about and into the part of the building where he was now standing. The smell was composed of night soil blended with the perfume Mary had told him was called Friendship's Garden that his old teacher used to apply liberally. Miss Vicks! He hadn't thought of her in years. She'd done the best she could with him, he had to hand it to her.

He remembered being rowed across the ornamental pond in a blue boat by a girl with fireflies in her hair as all the while Miss Vicks stood there keeping watch on the shore, her little red dachshund at her feet.

It was hard for Eddie to know which way to go. The corridor he was standing in extended to the right and the left for several yards before branching off in several directions. The wall on his right consisted mostly of windows facing out onto a courtyard filled with plants with very large leaves and a fountain; the wall to his left was hung with paintings. A pot of flowers, a sad-eyed child, a tilting house, a seascape—each painting was labeled with the artist's name and a brief description of how it had come to be painted. "I used to spend summers by the sea when I was very young," wrote the painter of the seascape, "but now I have to rely on my memories." Mary had made fun of a similar painting the night of the prom—this one even included the same body of water that looked nothing like water. He thought of the way the small of her back had felt under his hand, the way the knobs of her spine moved as they danced. He'd had her whole life in his hands—her whole life, and then nothing.

For a while he kept passing old men and women, most of them propelling themselves forward in wheelchairs or pushing walkers; only a few of the residents walked unassisted or with the help of a cane. Music began issuing from hidden speakers near the ceiling, occasionally interrupted by a voice announcing an activity or a birthday.

At some point Eddie found himself sitting in the dining room, staring into space. In one hand he was holding a yellow plastic toy of some kind; the other was resting flat on the arm of his chair. The dining room was empty at this hour. It was the worst hour of the day, the one that came after the big noonday meal was finished and the tables had been cleared and set for supper, the sounds from the kitchen growing harder to hear as if everything alive and capable of meaningful action had moved farther off like a population in retreat after a costly and decisive battle. There were no windows in the room; until the lights got turned on for supper there was almost no light in the room, except the light that came in off the hallway. Soon there would be no sound in the room, either, aside from the sound of Eddie drumming his fingers on the arm of his chair the way he used to when he was young and trying to think. Thought had never come easily to Eddie—he had always liked exercising his body better than exercising his mind.

Cindy XA had brought him the Yellow Bear earlier that morning; though she always came at the same time of day on the same day of the week, Eddie never failed to be surprised to see her. "How's Roy?" he would ask, and Cindy would inform him, gently, that Roy had passed away some time ago. He died in the announcer's box in the middle of a game—with his boots on, was the way Cindy put it.

"See if this will cheer you up," she had said, handing Eddie the bear. The fact that it was yellow threw Eddie off at first. Like many people he associated the color with sunshine and happiness, the old stories never having made much of an impression on him. Since he'd come to live in Woodard Village Eddie had been depressed, even after the kitchen named a drink in his honor. Rum Rocket, they told him it was called. Some of the people he lived with could still remember the way he used to be—like he had rocket boosters on his feet, everyone used to say.

He glanced up and noticed that Downie was pushing the same old woman toward the table where he was sitting. By now the room was filling with other residents, old people sitting in groups of four or six around tables covered with white tablecloths. It was a pleasant room with artificial floral centerpieces and aproned waitstaff, almost like a restaurant except all the waitstaff could perform CPR. Eddie put the bear on the table beside him. There was a plate in front of him with a piece of fish in the middle of it and a pile of peas at three o'clock and a pile of rice at noon but he had no appetite.

"What have you got there?" the old woman asked.

"You have to speak up," Downie said. "Otherwise he can't hear you."

"It's a combination plate," Eddie said. "I'm not deaf. I got one of these before and I didn't want to eat that one, either."

The old woman reached across the table and put her hand on Eddie's and held it and he could feel a tremor run through his whole body that either came from him or from her, he couldn't tell the difference.

He also couldn't tell where he was but he thought he could see approaching headlights. He seemed to remember something about a sorcerer named Body-without-Soul, but that was in a fairy tale he'd heard in his childhood. There was the smell of electricity; Eddie's hands were shaking so hard he couldn't pick up his napkin.

"See if he can manage this," the old woman said to Downie. She slid her bowl of broth across the table.

"Here, let me help you," Downie said, propping up Eddie, who had slid so far down in his chair he couldn't reach the table. "I'm going to break an egg into it to give it more body," Downie explained. "If I may?" He took the knife from the old woman's place setting without waiting for her to answer, then picked up the Yellow Bear and gave it a whack, separating the two halves of the shell and dropping the contents into Eddie's broth.

The room grew very quiet. Shadows padded along the walls, poured over Eddie like rain.

The old woman leaned closer and took off her sunglasses. "Uh oh," she said. "It looks like he's wet himself."

When she lifted her eyes to his he could see that they weren't cloudy the way he'd expected them to be but alive and silver and lit by the fire of her spirit, which, like the sun, couldn't be confronted directly but had to be filtered through the vitreous humor of her material self.

"You look like you just saw a ghost," the old woman said.

It was the last thing Eddie heard before his soul flew back into his body.

The Great Division

As FOR JANICE, SHE KEPT TREATING US LIKE GIRLS LONG after we were grown women. One of us went so far as to die—the last time we saw Janice was at the funeral. The service was over and people were milling around outside the chapel, some of them sobbing, some of them swatting at flies. It was a small chapel made of stone, the charming building in which Mary and Walter Woodard had exchanged their marriage vows and not far from the Italianate mansion where his father lived until he died or disappeared—even now there continued to be contention around this subject. On the other hand, everyone agreed Woodard Village had to be the greatest money-laundering venture ever.

What are you waiting for? Janice asked. She had climbed behind the wheel of one of those large beige vans mothers of six tended to drive, though as far as everyone knew Janice had remained childless. If you don't mind crowding together, she told us, I can fit you all in.

The reception was at the house where the deceased lived until she died; it was attached to the house in which a widower named O'Toole had gradually turned from man to ghost before escaping up the chimney. Most of us had gotten off the street years ago, though you could hardly call that an advantage. After a while the mere fact of being able to move from place to place supplanted the wish to conquer time but it was a poor substitute. Everyone knew the meaning of a thing didn't emerge until there'd been an ending and you could finally see how all the parts worked together.

I hope you remember what I told you about Pangaea, Janice said. The giant lump of stone, the giant sea? The black locket, the friendship rings, the socks? Because if we hadn't figured it out by now, it was the dead woman who'd been stealing things from us. Doll dresses, trading cards, you name it.

She always thought she was better than everyone, Janice said. You know that, don't you?

What we knew by now was that for as long as we'd known her Janice had suffered under the impression that everyone thought they were better than she was. Since the last time we'd been together Henry had gotten a divorce and married a former gymnast, and Janice had remarried twice. Her latest husband had been unable to attend the funeral—he needed to have some part of himself replaced.

Being better doesn't do you any good, Janice said. I hope you all know that by now.

As the sweet apple reddens on a high branch, high on the highest branch the apple pickers forgot—no, not forgot: were unable to reach. She didn't say it aloud, the way she would have before; instead the curly-haired girl nodded, even though Janice couldn't see her from where she sat. Janice was right, the girl thought. She was sitting in the way back, between the girl who had become a chemist and the girl who lived on a farm. The chemist was telling them that some molecules were unusual in that they were able to form bonds that couldn't be broken and were called exquisite, and that gold had the unusual advantage of being neither left- nor right-handed. Just like my goats! said the other girl. She had turned out prettier than everyone expected but also not so very bright.

Of course none of us were girls anymore. We weren't *really* old yet, but we were having trouble from time to time remembering things like what we'd had for dinner the night before. Most of us had married, some more than once. Some of us had children, one of us had a grandchild.

It's not easy to have a good marriage, Janice said—she seemed to be addressing herself. Then she sighed and honked her horn at something no one else could see. Had any of us heard about the worm addicted to grape leaves? she asked, letting up on the accelerator and giving another little honk of the horn. Of course we hadn't, as Janice well knew—no one had heard of it. There was a worm addicted to grape leaves, she continued, and suddenly it woke up. Call it a miracle, whatever, something woke it up and it wasn't a worm anymore. It was the whole vineyard, and the orchard too, the fruit, the trunks, an ever-expanding joy that didn't need to devour anything.

She sped up, driving the van down the third of the three hills, past the school and the water tower and across the railroad bridge.

I can't remember the last time I was back here, someone said. She'd married a foreigner and had developed a bit of an accent.

Worms? said someone else. Is she talking about worms now?

I would kill for a drink, said the chemist.

Amazingly, there was one parking spot left at the end of the street up near the Avenue; Janice began the complicated job of maneuvering the van into it.

We used to sit there, the curly-haired girl said, on those very steps. Very eyes, she recalled Janice saying and someone asking, what are very eyes? It might have been the dead woman but she couldn't be sure. That's where I traded everything away, the girl thought. Night had been falling. The stars had just been coming out though really they'd been there all along. They were there now behind the bright blue banner that was the sky.

The dead woman's parents had money, Janice said; I wonder what became of it? They wanted lots of children, more or less in the spirit of plantation owners wanting slaves, but they only got the one. After grade school they sent her off to a boarding school where she wore a blue uniform and everyone studied the classics, the kind of place you'd go if you wanted to learn Greek so you could read things like those poems you were always so keen on. She caught the curly-haired girl's eye in the rearview mirror. But the poor thing was never much of a student, was she? I heard she played cover point on the JV lacrosse team and she enjoyed history, but only because she had a crush on the teacher.

In grade school she could do the times tables faster than anyone, said the chemist.

That's just memorizing, said Janice. In fourteen hundred ninety-two Columbus sailed the ocean blue. No big deal. Anyone can memorize. You, me. Chimps, even. What I'm saying is she didn't have brains.

She's dead, said the smallest of the little sisters who'd grown into a large woman with a flourishing business of her own. She was our friend. Why can't someone say something nice about her?

We'd spent a lot of time together a long time ago but Janice was right. Like Pangaea, when the parts came back together, the coastline of Asia didn't dovetail with South America, just as you couldn't make a pair anyone would want to trade for out of Pinkie and a horse. Some continents moved faster and farther than others. The one who'd married a foreigner became a famous opera singer.

After boarding school she went to college, Janice continued. She went to a good school, but that was because her parents had money. The kind of school where they dance around a maypole but also volunteer at soup kitchens. That kind of place. She was still a whiz at memorizing facts; everyone's always been hot for facts. Dates, names, you know what I mean. She majored in history. She knew loads of things. She knew the War of the Roses didn't have anything to do with roses. She knew about all the wars. Don't major in history if you don't want to hear about wars. She knew about General Wolfe scaling the Heights of Abraham. She knew about the atom bomb. She knew secret restricted data about brown-skinned people being used as guinea pigs after the Castle Bravo accident. She even knew about the Know-Nothings.

I hate this, the opera singer said. This is boring. She was standing toward the back of the group, trying to speak sotto voce, but Janice overheard her.

History *is* boring, Janice concurred, undaunted as usual. It's not like the Ride of the Valkyries. It's what comes *before* history that isn't boring. She hummed a little, *hoyotoho, hoyotoho*. Prophecy, she said. Prophecy isn't boring.

Getting old had agreed with Janice, bringing her bones closer to the surface. For the funeral she'd donned a plain black dress and was wearing her hair in a twist—she looked a little like a sibyl.

We should go inside, said the chemist. It'll seem weird if we stay out here any longer.

Everyone began moving up the steps, closer to the front door. Summer was over but the trees had yet to let go of their leaves. The air was still warm but it had a cool blade in it, sharpening the shadows of the sycamores. The women could hear the sound of music coming through the open windows of the deceased's house—someone was playing the piano. They could also hear the sound of many people speaking all at once but keeping their voices down, in deference to the dead.

She always wanted to be a good girl, Janice reminded us, turning from where she stood at the door, her hand on the knob.

I thought you said she was the one who stole things, someone said.

Sure, Janice said. She did. But nothing really valuable.

That locket was a family heirloom, said someone else.

Be that as it may, Janice replied. She didn't finish the thought.

What was important was that the deceased was no different from the rest of us. She went to school and she said her prayers and eventually all the bad things she never allowed herself to do blended together inside her into a feeling that wouldn't come to the surface like the bubble in the carpenter's level that was still down there in what used to be her father's cellar workshop.

If you don't believe me, go look, Janice said. That's what happens to girls when they have the wish to be good, so good they almost can't be seen.

I heard she was pretty tall when she died, said the farmer. I heard they had to cut her feet off to fit her in the coffin.

Oh for heaven's sake, said the chemist.

That's just a fairy tale, said someone else.

The opera singer began to sing: Light she was and like a fairy and her shoes were number nine. For a moment her voice took us with it as it flew skyward, before dropping us back down to the ground.

Inside the house was extremely hot, even with the changing season and the windows open. Whoever was playing the piano was proficient but musically oblivious, speeding through a series of maudlin tunes as if there were no tomorrow.

That trip to Italy was the high point of her life, a family member was saying, pointing to a large framed print of Michelangelo's *David* hanging over the piano.

I had no idea, said the opera singer. Like the rest of us, she was visibly brighter now that she had a glass of whiskey in her hand. I thought the only place she went was to the shore, like everyone else around here.

It was a tour, Janice said. Milan to Florence to Venice to Rome. She met a man in Florence and took him back to her hotel room with her. He wasn't as handsome as David but he was Italian and, more important, he had all the working parts. During the night bats got into the room through the shutters and flew around and around up near the ceiling. The hotel had very high ceilings—at first she and the man tried standing on the bed and using pillowcases to chase the bats out the windows, but after a while they gave up. In the morning the bats had curled themselves into little balls in the agapanthus leaves of the ceiling fixture and the man was gone.

An Italian lover, said the opera singer. Who would have thought it.

That's why she worked for a travel agent, Janice said. Because of that tour. Every day when she went to work she sat in an office with posters of exotic places hanging on the walls. Not just London and Paris. Nepal. Machu Picchu. You get all kinds of discounts if you work for a travel agent. But she never took advantage of them. She went to her college reunions and she went to the shore and that was about it. Until she came down with lung cancer she was pretty healthy. She didn't smoke. She did some yoga. I think she was in a book club for a while, but she quit when they stopped talking about the books and started talking about personal things like their feelings.

We never went to the shore, said the farmer. We couldn't afford to. Every summer I'd watch you all drive away in your station wagons. Then I'd go up to my room and play My Little Pony. I was heartbroken but I never told anyone except the ponies. Of course they couldn't hear a thing.

Like that poor girl left behind by the Aquanauts, said someone else. That poor girl they left all alone.

Right, said the chemist. What about her?

By this time they had moved through the living room and dining room and kitchen and out the back door into the little yard. In the yard on the other side of the stockade fence someone was burning leaves.

I thought this time the story was going to be about the Great Division, said the opera singer. I have to admit I'm disappointed.

You wouldn't think there'd be enough leaves yet to make a pile, the farmer said. She rose on her tiptoes to look over the fence.

Janice accepted a scallop wrapped in bacon from a tray offered by a serving person wearing a tight black dress and a small white apron. Disappointed? she said. What do you mean disappointed?

Just that this time nothing's happening, not like with the Rain of Beads or the Horsewomen or the Aquanauts, the opera singer said.

I don't know what you're talking about. Janice had unwrapped the scallop and was looking at it critically. Sometimes they weren't real scallops but skate cut in the shape of scallops with a cookie cutter. The way you could tell was if there was a hinge.

That was the important thing, Janice explained—the hinge not only being the place where a real scallop attached

itself to its shell, but also the place where you could go forward and back with equal ease.

A lot of things happened, Janice said. Weren't you listening? The way things happen to all of us. At some point the
dead woman stopped being a child; she put her foot down.
She went to school, she went to Italy, she went to work, she
got sick and died. Some people live to be older than she did.
Some people get married or have families. You could even
be highly thought of by a lot of people before you die. You
could be famous.

She means the opera singer, thought the curly-haired
woman. Everyone knows who she is even if they hate opera.
She's over the hill and she's still terrific-looking and she
hasn't had any work done. I *hate* you, thought the curly-
haired woman, but she didn't, not really. Out of all the girls
she'd grown up with, the opera singer had always been one
of her favorites.

For a period the curly-haired girl had enjoyed limited
notoriety as a poet but her books had never garnered what
you'd call widespread critical acclaim. She had lived here,
she had lived there. At some point she moved to be near her
little sister, who'd ended up happily married to a man who
owned his own grocery store, and after that she didn't move
around anymore. She'd had lovers but she'd never been
married; she'd known happiness and she'd known sorrow.
She was not so very different, in other words, from the dead
woman, except for the fact that she was alive. When Janice
called to tell her the news she'd been having one of those
boring dreams that pass through your subconscious like an
endless train of boxcars. She woke up drenched with sweat
and filled with dread and the phone was ringing. The first
of you to go, Janice had said, and the next thing the curly-
haired girl knew she was crying as if her heart would break,

despite the fact that she hadn't known the deceased all that well, not even long ago when they were girls together.

What she means is nothing *interesting* happened, said the farmer. She looked over at the opera singer to make sure she'd got it right.

Exactly, the opera singer said. She was staring toward the back of the yard where there was a little birdbath that had a statue of St. Francis standing in the middle of the water, looking down at it, watching a gray-brown bird. What became of all the interesting parts, she asked, things like getting taken up into the sky, or being part horse, or being immortal? This story doesn't have anything like that going on in it. In this story things like that aren't even possible. She cleared her throat and began to sing: You are lost and gone forever, dreadful sorry, Clementine.

Well, duh, Janice said. That's the *point*. Haven't you been paying attention? That's the Great Division, like I was saying. That's the hinge. On one side, St. Francis there receives the stigmata. On the other side, he isn't even a saint. He's a stonemason, something along those lines. She took a seat at the patio table and lit a cigarette. Maybe he gets lung cancer, she said, blowing out smoke. Stranger things have been known to happen.

I don't understand, said the chemist.

The farmer was looking at the flowers growing around the birdbath. The deceased had a green thumb, she told us, a doting expression on her face.

Anyone can grow zinnias, someone said. Zinnias, marigolds—who cares.

But I'm *serious*, the opera singer persisted. What about those other parts? The parts before it gets boring? There must have been some parts like that in her life.

Oh, honey, Janice said. She opened her arms wide and waved them around in an attempt to take in all of us, the backyard, the birdbath, the sycamore trees, the whole wide world. They're over, she said. They've been over for forever. Look at you, she said. Just look at you! What do you expect? It was your past too—how could you forget it?

What's so bad about zinnias? the curly-haired girl wondered. What's so bad about being brightly colored at a time when everything else is turning dark?

I want to go home now, she thought. She didn't know what she meant by home, only that it wasn't here. As usual no one was paying attention to her and her heart was heavy because of her failure. The serving person returned carrying a platter of miniature crab cakes. A second serving person appeared with a bottle of red wine. It doesn't matter, the girl thought. She opened the gate and was surprised at how quiet it was on the other side of the stockade fence. The house across the driveway looked empty, the windows dark, the curtains drawn. It looked like no one had ever lived there but of course that wasn't true—it was the house she'd grown up in. Maybe everyone was at the reception.

She hadn't had that much to drink but even so she was careful as she started down the drive. She was wearing high-heeled shoes and on this side of the street the driveways were very steep. Soon it would be night; soon it would be autumn. Soon it would be winter and then it would be cold.

It wasn't until she arrived on the sidewalk that she realized how late it had gotten to be. Most of the streetlights were broken but one of the ones that still worked was shining down on a big gray hare. The hare was hesitating in the center of the street on its hind legs, its front paws lifted and folded neatly against its chest. The girl spoke to it softly. Here, boy, here, but it just looked at her in exasperation before hopping off down the sidewalk in front of the houses on the opposite side of the street.

Hop hop hop. In another moment down went the curly-haired girl after it, never once considering how in the world she was going to get back again.

The houses on the street were all the same, it was just the people living in them who were different. The people who lived in the house where the girl had grown up had terrible taste in curtains. The brick of Janice's house had been painted pale blue. A little dog barked behind the door of a house where no dog had lived before and instead of the ivy plant in its bow window there was a gold lamp shaped like a naked woman. The large holly bush at the corner was gone.

The vacant lot, though—the vacant lot was still exactly the way it had been when the girl was a girl. She threw herself down on the short green grass, heedless of getting grass stains on her good silk skirt, and somehow tearing a hole in its hem with the heel of her shoe in the process.

The lot was a place you weren't supposed to linger in; in that way, also, nothing had changed. She tried to remember how long ago it had been that she'd felt the fluttering in her pocket that she'd thought was a common garden fairy but that turned out to be nothing more than her heart. It was so easy to get the two of them mixed up.

The sun began to get low and all the west was dyed red.

Uh oh, said her friend the lustrous black ant.

When the Space Drift finally took place it was like everything—everything that is and has been and always will be—became for a moment like a huge thick velvet curtain, and everything that ever considered itself to be separate from anything else no longer was but only just for that moment, the moment of the Drift, while space was carrying away time in its soft dark folds like a lover.

Suddenly the curly-haired girl perceived that the grass was growing up between her and where she'd been. It had long spearlike leaves, it pushed up long pipes of green stem, and they whistled. She began to have a curious feeling as if all of this had already happened, and then half her sorrow faded into wonder, and the feeling grew upon her that these things had happened a long time ago. She drew a little nearer. It was a long time ago, she repeated.

Acknowledgments

Thank you to the Bogliasco Foundation and the Lannan Foundation for their support.

"Descent of the Aquanauts" appeared in *Conjunctions*.

"The Four Horsewomen" appeared in *Mischief and Mayhem*.

"The Rain of Beads" appeared in *Little Star*.

"Through the Wormhole" appeared in *New England Review*.

A very different version of "Body-without-Soul" appeared in *My Mother She Killed Me, My Father He Ate Me*, edited by Kate Bernheimer (Penguin, 2010).

A part of "Yellow Bear" appeared in *Significant Objects*, edited by Joshua Glenn (Fantagraphics, 2012).

I also want to thank Louise Glück for her help with the manuscript.

The novel is haunted by the ghosts of Sappho, *Mopsa the Fairy*, and "The New Mother."

KATHRYN DAVIS is the author of six previous novels, the most recent of which is *The Thin Place*. Her other books are *Labrador*, *The Girl Who Trod on a Loaf*, *Hell*, *The Walking Tour*, and *Versailles*. She has received a Kafka Prize for fiction by an American woman, the Morton Dauwen Zabel Award from the American Academy of Arts and Letters, and a Guggenheim Fellowship. In 2006 she won the Lannan Foundation Literary Award. She is the senior fiction writer on the faculty of the writing program at Washington University.

Duplex has been set in Adobe Caslon Pro, a typeface drawn by Carol Twombly in 1989, and based on the work of William Caslon (c. 1692–1766), an English engraver, punchcutter, and typefounder. Book design by Ann Sudmeier. Composition by BookMobile Design and Digital Publisher Services, Minneapolis, Minnesota. Manufactured by Friesens on acid-free 100 percent postconsumer wastepaper.